"Pete had been like Christmas, something that came along once in a while. You couldn't have Christmas every day.... Just for a while it looked as though maybe they could have Christmas every day, that maybe they could all stay together forever, but it had been dumb of him to think that. In real life that didn't happen."

Tommy Bridges knows that "Christmas," and the joy of almost having a father, are over for him. His mother Susan has quarreled with Pete, and she and Tommy are on their own now, in Los Angeles. While Susan auditions for TV commercials, Tommy is left to wander about the new neighborhood and yearn for the good days: the warmth and security of living with Pete in the cottage on the beach, the fun of being out in the old boat, *Lazy Gal,* while Pete dived for abalone.

One day Tommy discovers an abandoned estate in the hills overlooking the city and finds camping there two people as lonely as himself. Dropouts Joel and Little Horse become Tommy's friends and help him to begin to see that there are many kinds of fathers.

Stuart Buchan's novel movingly depicts the incompleteness of a boy's life and the risk he takes to make it whole.

when we lived with pete

STUART bUCHAN
WHEN WE LiVEd
WiTH pETE

Charles Scribner's Sons
New York

Copyright © 1978 Stuart Buchan

Library of Congress Cataloging in Publication Data
Buchan, Stuart.
When we lived with Pete.
SUMMARY: Needing a father, a young boy tries
to repair the broken relationship between his
widowed mother and her friend Pete.
[1. Single-parent family—Fiction.   2. Family
life—Fiction]   I. Title.
PZ7.B875Wh   [Fic]   77-16440
ISBN 0-684-15493-5

1 3 5 7 9 11 13 15 17 19 V/C 20 18 16 14 12 10 8 6 4 2

Printed in the United States of America

For
CHRISTOPHER BREWER

when we lived with pete

1

"WHEN WE LIVED with Pete . . ." Tommy said.

"We don't live with Pete anymore," his mother interrupted before he could finish. She spoke quietly but he could tell she was upset. "We live by ourselves now. In our own apartment. And we just have to make the best of it."

He had been going to say that when they lived with Pete there was always something to do. Pete had a boat and made his money diving for abalone, which was a neat way to make a living. When they lived with Pete, Tommy went out on the boat on weekends. Pete did the diving and Tommy cleaned the abalone shells and kept the boat tidy. Most days they went out at first light just as the dawn was tracing a pink line along the Santa Barbara Channel, and they stayed out there until five or six o'clock. They would come back when the wind was rising and the waves had white crests on them that bucked Pete's old boat and threw spray in their faces. Then they took the abalone to the Castanola fish canners, maybe keeping some for themselves, and when they got home it was seven, maybe eight o'clock, and Tommy was so tired he could barely sit up for dinner.

The days just went when they lived with Pete. Now they dragged on. Tommy was hardly ever tired now, real tired, tired from a hard day working with Pete. These days he was just bored, and when he went to bed he lay awake thinking about how it used to be when they lived with Pete. Sometimes the thinking hurt and he'd want to cry a little but he didn't. He wasn't afraid of crying. Pete had told him that lots of guys cried, even grown men sometimes when they were hurting bad, so it was all right for a boy of thirteen to cry if he had to. That wasn't why he didn't cry. He didn't cry because he knew his mom would hear him where she was sleeping in the next room on the fold-down couch and if she heard him cry, she'd cry. Sometimes she cried anyway, but she tried to muffle her face in her pillow so Tommy wouldn't hear.

His mom missed Pete as much as Tommy did, but that didn't seem to make any difference. She still couldn't get back together again with Pete, not after the fight.

"I have an audition at four. Will you be O.K.?"

Tommy pulled his T-shirt over his head. "Sure. Will you be late?"

"No. I don't think so. It's a toothpaste commercial. They'll just look at my teeth like I'm a horse or something and say yes or no. No lines."

Tommy laughed. "They can tell how old a horse is from his teeth. Maybe you better not show them yours, Mom."

His mother cuffed him on the ear lightly. "Listen, you," she said. "You have one young gorgeous mother, you know that? I'm not afraid to show anybody my teeth. Which is more than I can say for you, I'll bet. When did you last clean your teeth?"

"Last night."

"Ho, ho. Last week, more likely. In you go. Five minutes at the sink for that remark about my age. And clean them well," she called as she gathered up his clothes from the floor and went out of the bedroom. "Up and down, and not just a couple of fast strokes and a lot of water."

Tommy went into the bathroom, smoothing his hair flat. It bounced right back again, red and curly like a fluffy Brillo pad all over his head. He had freckles and green eyes and looked like his dad. He didn't remember his dad. The picture in the front room of a young man in the uniform of a naval officer was all he knew of him. Sometimes he stared at the picture for a long time trying to figure out what it would have been like if his dad had lived, but all he saw was that young guy in the white uniform, smiling at the camera. You couldn't really tell anything from a picture, not much anyway, just that he had red curly hair too and looked like he'd been a happy guy.

"What are you going to do today?" his mom asked, coming back into the bathroom. "You going to swim in the pool?"

"Naw. There's always lots of old people around the

(5)

pool. They get mad if I splash or make any noise. They just want to sit there and read newspapers and listen to that goofy music. I'm going to go out and spook around."

His mom smoothed his hair down again and it bounced right back. She left her hand on the back of his neck. "You be careful, honey. This isn't the best neighborhood in the world. I wish I could come up with something better, but right now this has got to be it. You stay off the boulevard. Those are real bad types down there. Don't you ever go anywhere with any of those kids."

"When you're a star, Mom, we'll live in Beverly Hills and have our own pool and you won't have to do commercials," Tommy said, and he saw his mother's eyes light up.

"You bet we will. You wait and see. But first I've got to get that damn toothpaste job today. Who knows, maybe some agent will see me and say, 'Wow, that chick sure has great teeth. I gotta sign her up!' "

She followed Tommy out into the living room. The sofa bed was folded back, the pillows put away on the shelf of the front closet. All the furniture came with the apartment and it wasn't much. It wasn't like waking up at Pete's up the coast, where the furniture wasn't much either but you didn't notice it, because just outside the window was the beach and you always got the sound of the sea all night long. You could hear the traffic on the Pacific Coast Highway in the day, but if you stopped and listened you'd hear the surf crashing in, even over the sound of the traffic behind the shack, and that made everything great.

Outside the apartment building all you got was dog

filth on the sidewalk and two blocks away Hollywood Boulevard and all the weirdos.

But that was what they had right now and he knew his mom was doing what she could. Most of all they had each other. They didn't have anybody else, but they had each other and that was plenty. They looked after each other.

Except, of course, for a while they had had Pete too, but Tommy didn't want to think about that. Pete had been like Christmas, something wonderful that came along once in a while. You couldn't have Christmas every day. Nobody had Christmas every day. Just for a while it looked as though maybe they could have Christmas every day, that maybe they could all stay together forever, but it had been dumb of him to think that. In real life that didn't happen. In real life you just got Christmas sometimes and the rest of the time you watched out for the filth on the sidewalk.

He checked that he had the door key to the apartment and the key to the building on the string around his neck. He tucked them under the neck of his T-shirt.

"Bye, Mom."

"You have a good day," she called from the bathroom.

"You too. Good luck with the commercial."

He went down the two flights of stairs and out across the pool deck. The old people who lived in the other apartments were already out there, putting sun-tan oil on themselves and lying on the lounges. Someone had a transistor radio playing classical music. The people looked up at him suspiciously to see if he was coming down to swim and make some noise, but he went right on past and out

(7)

the main door of the building. He could almost hear them sigh with relief that he wasn't going to stay and swim, and that made him sore.

Outside the sidewalk was already hot and it was only ten o'clock in the morning. In the distance he could see the round Capitol Records building, built like a stack of records itself, and beyond that, already half hidden by the smog, the tall buildings of downtown L.A., like castles far away in the mist. Except smog isn't mist. Mist is clean and smog is dirty.

He sighed. Two blocks down there was the boulevard, and he didn't want to go there. He could take a bus and go out to Santa Monica to the beach. He checked his money. He had a dollar fifty-five. The bus was fifty cents each way. That wouldn't leave him much to eat on, and he might lose some money and then he wouldn't be able to get home.

He sighed again and looked around and said quietly, "L.A., you sure are one dump of a town," and while he was looking he saw, as he had seen lots of times since they moved into the apartment two weeks ago, the gates right up at the end of the street where the land sloped up into the hills behind Hollywood. The gates were beat-up and he knew that the sign he could just see from where he stood said NO TRESPASSING, but the chain that bound them together was rusted. His mom hadn't said anything about not going in there, but he knew without her telling him that he wasn't supposed to. All the same, here he was on a hot Friday in August and he didn't know anyone to go see, and the people at the pool didn't want him there, and, hell, he had to live, too. He was people even if he was a kid. They didn't want him around, but there wasn't anywhere for him to go, and if he thought about what it had been like when they lived up the coast he was going to be real upset all day; so he turned and walked up the street toward the gates, kind of mad and kind of excited, and thought, "It can't be worse in there than it is out here."

2

ONCE INSIDE THE gates he found a long winding driveway that was cracked and buckled. The little gatehouse, built of stone in the square shape of a turret, had a three-legged chair and some empty beer cases. Two rows of tall palm trees lined the driveway, the lower fronds hanging brown and dead, but the top fronds dark green, reaching up to the sunshine.

The road curved up into the hillside and was lost to his view twenty yards away. Down below near the gate there was a lot of underbrush, bushes that had overgrown and met each other with their branches, so it was like a small forest and the driveway a tunnel through it. He was only a few feet away from the street, but it seemed a lot quieter here behind the gates, silent almost, the leaves on the trees not moving and the branches casting a shadow over the road that made the air cool, too.

Tommy stood right where he was just beyond the gate for several minutes, listening to the quiet, trying to decide if he was scared or nervous, trying to decide if he should walk further on up the road and see where it went. After a while he decided he wasn't scared. He was alert, like Pete always said you had to be when you dived for abalone shells, going down fifty feet, sometimes without a tank, and all you had was the air in your lungs; there wasn't any room for trouble and there were sharks out there in the channel sometimes, but Pete wasn't scared. "Not scared, Tommy," he said when Tommy asked. "I'm alert, that's what I am. A man can't let himself be scared when he's out there or he'd never go down, and he'd always know that the reason he didn't dive was because he was scared of something that might not even be there, and he wouldn't think much of himself if he let something like that frighten him away from doing what he really wants to do. But I'm alert, that's what I am, because I know I'm taking a chance down there, but it's what I want to do, what I like to do. So I do it, but I dive as carefully as I can, and at the first sign of trouble I get the hell out of there fast." And then Pete would laugh at himself, that big laugh he had, and Tommy would laugh too at the thought of Pete getting the hell out of the water fast because he was afraid of something.

Beyond the tunnel made by the trees the land opened up. The gate was at one end of a canyon and the road wound up until it forked, one branch going left, following the curve of the canyon wall, a narrow strip that meandered away into the distance until it was lost from sight.

The other branch went straight ahead for a while and then doglegged sharply right, up toward a stone wall that loomed above the road like the base of a fortress. The bottom of the canyon was overgrown with grass that was hay-high and as bleached dry as a Kansas wheatfield. There were overgrown gardens, too. Climbing roses rambled up the canyon wall. Exotic trees that Tommy had never seen before grew all about, trees whose trunks snaked out along the ground and entangled with other trees, just like vines, except they were thick and had wild striped leaves and from some of them purple flowers hung down like bells.

He kept on walking, choosing the path that went to the right because he could see where that would lead to, high up there but not too far away, like Pete taking a dive but taking care. All the sounds of the city were gone now. Now it was like being in the country, and he heard birds call, and he jumped once when the grass right by his feet moved suddenly, making a dry sound like a snake. A tiny lizard ran out into the sunlight, blinked at him, and scurried back under the bushes.

Where the road doglegged to the right, it turned steeply upward. The pavement stopped and the road became a path, dry dirt with a furrow running down the center where water had run off. The palm trees stopped at the end of the driveway, and now the path was edged with cacti as tall as he was. They sat like sentinels along the edge of the path with leaves like spearheads. Someone must have planted them there a very long time ago, because they were huge, bigger than any cacti he'd ever seen in the desert. The leaves were a light green color and some of the old ones had died and fallen off. The dry husks lay along the path.

Tommy followed the path upward and saw what looked like a bank of vines thickly overgrown, but as he looked closer he saw a chain-link fence, and when he got closer to a gap in the vines he was looking down into an old abandoned tennis court that couldn't be seen from below. The court was built right on a ledge off the side of the canyon wall, and the vines were ivy that had been planted along the fence to stop the balls from falling over into the path below. The ivy had grown over the fence and crept along the court itself, edging forward, making a pattern on the brown surface. There were two posts, and some ragged threads that had once been a net.

He got an eerie feeling looking down into that ruined tennis court, and he took another deep breath and looked up at the sun and then over at the other road on the other wall of the canyon. He had a better view of it now but he still couldn't see where it went. The canyon wound back and forth, up and up, and the road followed it away into the distance. Down below, where he couldn't see before, there were ruins of two small buildings, one down near the gate behind the bank of overgrown roses and another hidden back below the far road. The building near the gate was falling down, but it still had part of a roof. All that was left of the other one was a chimney stack sticking up like a big barbecue pit, that and some stones scattered about nearby.

He turned back to the dirt path and followed it a little farther. He could see that he was coming to the end of the path. Ahead there was a broad expanse of sky and a flat mesa of land. As he got closer he saw the ruins of another small building and then suddenly a huge hole in the ground, rectangular, with concrete walls across which someone had scrawled graffiti: *Viva Pepe, Marilyn & Chuck, Power to the People.* The words were uneven, letters starting small and ending big, scratched on the concrete with charcoal. Now that he was right on the rim of the hole he could see that it had once been a swimming pool but now was filled halfway up the sides with dead leaves, tree branches, rags scattered here and there. The space around had once been a pool deck. The grass underfoot had come up through the cracks in the concrete and crept across the deck until it covered almost the whole area. The ruined building had been a cabana for changing. There was an old car seat sticking half out from under a collapsed wall, and more torn rags nearby, but these looked newer. The rags in the bottom of the old pool were dirty, but the ones by the car seat were still brightly colored as though they hadn't been out in the sun and rain too long.

He turned away from that view and looked over the pool; from here he could see the whole city. The Capitol Records building was down there, very small, and the pagoda roof of Mann's Chinese Theatre. There was the strange building that they called the Magic Castle, where the Hollywood magicians had their club, and way far away was the downtown area with City Hall and the other tall buildings.

"I'm right on top of the world up here," he said aloud.

The silence of the place was getting to him. After so much city noise, it made him nervous for things around him to be so quiet. He wanted to jump when branches rubbed together in the hot breezes. So he spoke aloud, his voice sounding weird and rusty as though it, like the pool and the tennis court, hadn't been used for a long time.

The city lay spread out below him. If he looked the other way, he bet he could see Beverly Hills and maybe even the ocean, maybe even Catalina Island. He turned in the other direction, narrowing his eyes to see better into the sun, and as he did he realized with a shock that he could feel right down into his sneakers that he was being watched. A boy had crept out from under the collapsed wall of the pool house and sat cross-legged on the old car seat, with his hands on his knees, staring hard at Tommy, and he was smiling.

For a few long seconds neither of them said anything. Finally the boy spoke, his words coming very slowly, his voice strangely deep for someone so young. "You're lucky you came this way," he rasped. "If you'd taken the other road you'd have met the Indian."

3

THE BOY HAD long blond hair, was dressed in a blue denim shirt and Levis, and looked to be a couple of years older than Tommy. Fifteen maybe.

"You live there?"

The boy didn't answer him right away. At length he said, "I used to live in Beverly Hills. I ran away."

"No kidding!" Tommy said. "You ran away from Beverly Hills?" He couldn't imagine anyone running away from Beverly Hills where everybody had their own pool and tennis court and the kids had their own cars. His mom said that when she got famous and rich they'd live in Beverly Hills and Tommy would have his own car when he was sixteen to drive to school.

"Yeah," the boy said. "I and my dad have had it. I'm not going to take any more from him, so I ran away." He stood up and Tommy could see that he was really thin. The boy went over to a faucet near the ground. He washed his face with the water and rinsed out his mouth. He shook his head like a big dog and his hair fell back into place more neatly.

"Now you live here, huh?" Tommy said.

The boy looked back at Tommy as though he'd forgotten Tommy was there. "It's O.K.," he said. "But you've got to watch out for the Indian. He lives up the other way and he's as mean as hell."

He gestured across the canyon at the winding road. Tommy followed the sweep of his hand, wondering where the road went. It wound on and on. From here he could see that it went still further than he had thought. It went right to the top of the canyon and ran along the rim like a ledge. From here he could see what looked like a wall running by the road at the top.

"Does the Indian own this place?"

The boy scowled. He turned away and leaned against his shelter. "Nobody owns it," he said. "Not really. A real rich guy from back East used to own it, but he got divorced and the judge told him to give his wife a lot of money—but he wouldn't, so he just up and left. He can't ever come back to California if he doesn't give his wife the money. So he can't come back here. He must be real rich," he said. After a pause, he added, "He must be real mean, too. As mean as the Indian, I guess, to let this place go. He must've hated his wife real bad to give up this place just so he wouldn't have to pay her."

The two boys stood looking around at the deserted estate. Tommy figured it was getting close to lunchtime. The climb had taken him a long time.

"You got any money?" the boy asked him.

Something in how the boy spoke scared Tommy just a little bit, just for a minute. He'd heard about kids that got mugged. But this boy didn't look like any mugger. He looked like the kids who played volleyball on the beach.

"I got a dollar fifty-five," he said.

"I'm as hungry as hell," the boy said, but he didn't look at Tommy as he said it. He still looked away out across the canyon. Tommy could have asked him down to the apartment for lunch, but something told him not to do that. Instead he said, "I'll loan you seventy-five cents."

The boy looked at him then. "O.K." he said, but he didn't say it as though he were grateful. It didn't sound like thanks. It sounded as if he thought Tommy should be glad to give him the money, and right away Tommy was sorry he'd said he'd loan him the seventy-five cents. "Can't get much for seventy-five cents," the boy said. "But it's better than starving, I guess." He looked at Tommy, just stood and looked with his hands in the front pockets of his jeans cowboy-style until Tommy knew he was waiting for the money. Tommy fumbled in his pockets for the money and counted out the seventy-five cents. The boy took it without a word.

"We can go down to the Cup," he said, leading the way across the grass-grown platform.

"Down there?" Tommy asked, looking back down at the road. He was still hot from the climb. He didn't want to have to go all the way down again now. He wanted to look around this strange estate. He wasn't hungry himself.

Something of his reluctance must have come into his voice, for the other boy said, "Not all the way down the road. That's the long way."

On the side of the platform that faced out across the city he walked right toward some bushes, bushes with yellow flowers like brushes on the end of the branches, and jumped right out into space—at least that's what it looked like to Tommy. Tommy felt his heart stop as though he'd just had the fright of his life, and then pound up again. He ran forward and saw that where the bushes were shaking, the hillside sloped up not quite so steeply, and the boy was sliding down a narrow path on the seat of his jeans. He was sliding down what looked like a mighty dangerous path, and he knew how to do it. Tommy could tell from the way he grabbed hold of certain bushes on the way down, reaching out for them without looking, to steady himself and slow himself down a bit. It looked as though he were trying to leave Tommy behind, and another feeling of anger swept over Tommy at the thought that he'd been ripped off for his money and now was to be left behind.

So taking a deep breath, he leaped into the bushes and felt himself skidding a lot faster than he had intended. He didn't know where the bushes were to grab onto, and once he started down, the momentum carried him faster and faster, the leaves of the bushes slapping his face so that he had to half close his eyes. He sat right down on the dirt halfway down and took the last hundred yards of the slide on his behind.

But he came sliding out onto the cracked concrete of the driveway just a few feet behind the boy, and he even managed to stand up quickly without looking half as shaken as he really felt.

He could tell that the boy hadn't expected him to get down so fast and was sort of impressed. He looked at Tommy now, really looked at him the way you do when you think someone might be all right, might be a friend or important or something, and you want to see him properly because you want to remember him.

Tommy dusted himself off. The boy watched him. "I'll show you how to get down there," he said, looking Tommy in the eyes as he spoke, something he hadn't done before. Before, he'd always looked away as though he didn't really care whether Tommy was there, or else he would glance at Tommy quickly. He was speaking to Tommy now like a buddy—a partner, as Pete would say. "I've got a way that I go. It's easier."

They had come out of the bushes right by the gate. The little gatehouse with the three-legged chair and the empty beer cartons was there. The boy reached forward and slapped Tommy lightly on the arm. "C'mon," he said. "Let's go get something to eat before I perish right here before your eyes," and he smiled suddenly, the first time he'd smiled, and the smile was almost as big a shock as seeing him jump off the cliff. When he smiled he looked like a different boy. He looked like the happiest guy on earth and made Tommy feel like that too. And when he smiled something else happened: he didn't look older anymore. He looked real young, like a kid almost.

The boy pushed his way past the gatehouse and Tommy followed, feeling that the day was working out pretty terrific. When he came in here a couple of hours ago he was feeling low. Now here he was, just a couple of hours later, and even rotten old L.A. looked pretty good. "When you've got a partner," Pete used to say, "nothin' looks bad. But partners, they're not easy to find. A guy makes maybe four, five real friends in his whole life if he's lucky, and you never know when it's gonna happen. You can't go looking for a friend. All you can do is prepare yourself so you're the type of guy someone would want to be friends with. And then you wait and if you're lucky someone comes along and you know right away that you've got a friend. That's about the best feeling in the world, the feeling you get when you've just met a friend."

4

HOLLYWOOD BOULEVARD WAS a dump. The bronze stars sunk into the sidewalk with the names of famous actors were dirty with gum and spit and worse.

Tommy's new friend moved fast along the sidewalk toward the restaurant, stepping in between the tourists. He looked at Tommy and said, "You'll pass."

"For what?"

"You don't look like a runaway," he said. "If you look like a runaway the cops'll stop you. You look too clean." Then he looked at himself in the reflection from the shop windows and tossed his blond hair again.

"They ever stop you?" Tommy asked.

"No. I don't look like a runaway," the boy said, and added, "Not yet."

As they walked along the sun-baked sidewalk, Tommy

looked more closely at the other kids. Some of them were neat and clean but most of them looked kind of dirty. Their jeans were old and torn. Their hair needed washing.

"That's what a runaway looks like," the boy said, pointing out a kid who was leaning against a street corner. The kid looked real tired, exhausted. His face was thin. He had circles under his eyes. He didn't look very happy. "After a while runaways get to look like that. It's a tough life."

They came to the Gold Cup Restaurant and went in. The restaurant was as busy as the sidewalk. Most of the crowd were teenagers, but there were some older men too. The young didn't seem to have anything to do or anyplace to go. They sat in the booths with a look to them that said they were just waiting for something to happen. The older men came in and looked around and left quickly. Sometimes they talked to a kid.

The boy found them two seats at the counter. Tommy sat down beside him.

"How long you been on the road?" Tommy asked.

"Cool it," the boy said angrily. "Don't talk about that. If the cops get you they take you down to the station and ask you questions."

He ordered a hamburger from the black waitress behind the counter, and Tommy asked for a Coke. When she had left, the boy said, "I'm Joel—in case the cops ask. What's your name?"

"Tommy Bridges."

"Thanks a bunch, Tommy Bridges," Joel said, flashing

his smile again suddenly. "You're keeping me alive today."

Then he turned away and watched the action in the restaurant.

"How do these kids live?" Tommy asked, real low.

"They steal," Joel said. "Some hustle. Anything to get by, you know."

Tommy looked at Joel hard. He wondered if Joel had to steal. Joel must have known what Tommy was thinking because he said, "No, I haven't had to steal. Not yet."

The hamburger came and Joel ate it in three bites. Tommy was just starting on his Coke. "I've got fifty cents left," he said. "You want something else?"

Joel said, "Sometime I'll pay you back."

"O.K.," Tommy said, handing over the fifty-cent piece, keeping the quarter to pay for his Coke.

Joel had a piece of pie. The other kids came and went. Sometimes a waitress would walk over to a kid who was sitting over an empty coffee cup and tell him to get out. The waitresses didn't ask. They just told the kids, "You've been here long enough. Out." And the kid would stand up without a word and wander out into the sunlight with a no-place-to-go look, just walking.

Two police officers in uniform came into the restaurant and the place got busy, real quick. Kids started to talk to each other even if they didn't know each other. They laughed at nothing as though they had been talking before the cops arrived. Nobody looked at the cops. Nobody except Tommy, that is. He looked right at them to see what they were going to do until Joel jabbed him in the ribs with his elbow and threw down the change for the burger and pie. "Pay for your Coke," he said, and Tommy put down his last quarter. Joel stood up very casually and said loudly, "You want to go see a movie?" Tommy only had one nickel left, so he didn't see how they could get into a movie, but before he could say anything Joel said, "I gotta be home by five. We could get into the two o'clock show down at the Paramount and I could get home in time for dinner," loud again, and Tommy knew he wasn't talking to him. Joel was talking to the officers. One of the officers turned to look at the boys as they walked past. He looked at them closely, up and down, and Tommy felt his heart give a jolt as though he had done something wrong, even though he hadn't. But he and Joel walked on past and the officers didn't stop them.

Out on the sidewalk Tommy could see that Joel was sweating. It was a hot day, but not hot enough for sweating. A line of beads had broken out on Joel's forehead.

"Let's get outa here," Joel said, and walked fast off down the side street.

"Joel what?" Tommy said.

"What do you mean?"

"What's your other name?"

They were a couple of blocks away by now, walking past a row of apartment buildings. Joel was relaxing. "I can't tell you," he said, slowing down. "My dad's real famous. If I told you his name you'd know who I was and you might tell someone. I can't trust you."

Tommy was hurt. He looked sideways at Joel to see if he recognized him. Because he was hurt, he said, "I don't care what your name is anyway. You don't have any manners. You're gross."

Joel stopped. "You bought me a hamburger," he said. "You didn't buy the right to tell me how to eat."

They walked along in silence for a while. Joel said eventually, "I don't want any friends."

"Oh," said Tommy. He didn't believe that. But he didn't want to get Joel angry, either. No matter what Joel said, Tommy already thought of him as a friend. "My mom makes me use good manners," he said. " 'Manners grease the tracks of the train of life,' she says."

"Your mom sounds like a real case," Joel said.

"She is not!"

"She must be," Joel said flatly, "if she lives in this town."

Tommy was getting angry now. "You live in this town," he said.

"Not much longer," the boy said. "I'm hitting the road soon as I get some bread together."

At the thought of losing his friend so fast, Tommy forgot his anger. "Where are you going?" he asked.

"Anywhere," Joel said. "Just so long as it's not here."

They had walked up to the gates of the estate. Joel didn't look very happy to be going back in there. He stood around outside the gates for a while as though he was working up the courage. "You coming in?" he asked.

Tommy looked down the street. There was no sign of anyone, no sign of his mom. "Sure," he said.

They climbed back around by the gatehouse. The silence of the estate hit Tommy right off. Just outside the gates you could hear traffic and sirens, feel the heat of the sidewalk right through your sneakers, but here just a few feet away it was cool and almost dead quiet.

"It's the trees," Joel said. "They block the sound and they make the road cool. This is country. That's what I want. I want country. No more city for this boy."

"I like the ocean," Tommy said.

"Yeah? You ever live there?"

Tommy didn't answer right away. He thought fast about Pete and all that. He didn't want to talk to just anyone about Pete. Pete was special. Pete was important. But he found himself saying, "I used to live at the ocean. When we lived with Pete."

"Oh, yeah?" Joel asked, nicely, softly, like he was interested. "Who's Pete?"

So Tommy told him about Pete, about living up the coast in the shack with Pete, about Pete's boat. He told him everything except why they weren't living with Pete anymore. And Joel didn't ask. Tommy liked him for that.

They walked all the way up the driveway to the broken pool while Tommy talked, and they sat down on the ledge and looked out over the city where the smog lay as thick as a winter blanket over the buildings. The afternoon got late while they talked and the sun got cool, and by the time Tommy had finished talking the afternoon was nearly gone.

"You ever miss your own dad?" Joel asked him.

Tommy screwed up his face to give a true answer. "I never knew my real dad," he said. "He died when I was real little. Sometimes I try to think what it would have been like if he'd lived, but that's not really missing him, is it? What I really miss," he said, saying it aloud for the first time to anyone, ever, "is Pete." He found it hurt even to say it, hurt as much as he had thought it would. "I miss Pete real bad," and to his shock he found that he was going to cry.

But Joel reached out and squeezed his shoulder and somehow that helped. The tears stopped before they got all the way out and Tommy swallowed hard a couple of times.

"What about you?" he asked when he could talk again. "Don't you miss your dad?"

Joel's face got hard suddenly. His eyes narrowed and his lips thinned. "I hate him!" he said viciously. "I hate that son-of-a-gun more than I hate anything in this life. If I never see him again it'll be too soon!"

5

"I WAS FEELING kinda down," his mother said, "because I didn't get the job, you know. I mean, there were about a hundred other girls there, some of them real young, eighteen, maybe younger even, and they all had these great teeth, so I knew right off that I was gonna have a tough time getting the job, but I figured that I might as well get started getting used to auditioning and all, so I stayed, and sure enough I just barely got into the office where all these guys are lined up around a table auditioning teeth, and they say, 'Thanks a lot, Miss Bridges'—I thought it'd be better to say I wasn't married or anything, you know—'but we're looking for a . . .' and he hesitated, sort of trying to find the right word, but I knew what he really wanted to say. He wanted to say 'younger woman.' He was just trying to let me down easy. He said, 'a different look,' and they opened the door for me again, and I was out there staring at the other hundred girls who were still waiting to go in. They knew that I hadn't got the job because I'd only been in there like three, four minutes after waiting five hours, just about, and suddenly I wanted to cry, so I walked right out of there with my head high and went into the nearest bar and ordered a drink."

Tommy felt sorry for his mom. They were driving up Coldwater to Mulholland in her old Mustang. The car futzed along, puffing out clouds of blue smoke behind. His mom kept looking at herself in the driving mirror every time she said that the other girls were younger than she was. She was looking at the lines beside her eyes and she was real down today, Tommy knew, or she wouldn't be telling him this. She didn't talk like this to him much, but now that they didn't live with Pete, she didn't have anyone else to talk to. Tommy didn't mind her talking to him like this. She was treating him like a grown-up. Trouble was, he didn't know what to say to her. He felt he should say something, but he didn't know what to say. He was afraid of saying something stupid like a kid would say, because then his mom would shut right up and she'd go on feeling bad but wouldn't have anyone to talk to about it. So he said nothing. He'd found that saying nothing wasn't such a bad idea. If he said nothing he found that sometimes people thought he was smarter than he was, when the truth was he just didn't know what to say.

"That's where I met Twink."

"In the bar?"

His mother looked at him quickly. "She's a waitress," she said. "She works there part time between acting jobs. She's really an actress, but work's short now, so she works in the bar. Her name's Twink Mondragon."

Tommy thought about that for a while. The old Mustang puffed over the top of the hill, turned left onto Mulholland, and caught its breath on the long winding road to Sherman Oaks.

"She's going to help me learn the ropes," his mother said. "Tell me how to get acting jobs, help me get an agent, that sort of stuff."

They turned off down the other side of the mountain into the valley. "She's along one of these side streets," his mom said. "Imagine, a swimming pool and everything."

They found the street and counted the numbers until they came to a small house with an Oriental moongate, with a little bridge that led to a round front door. "This is it," his mom said. "She told me it was Chinese."

She parked the car at the curb and they trudged over the bridge to the door. On close inspection they saw that there was no water in the cement basin underneath and that the house needed painting. The doorbell rang inside like a trumpet, loud and clear. They stepped back from the door and waited, but nobody came. They waited three or four minutes, and then his mom reached out and nervously pushed the doorbell again. The trumpet blared out like a marching band inside, but before it could play the whole chord, the door was pulled open and the sound stopped abruptly.

Standing in the doorway was a short middle-aged lady with bright red hair all messed up, and her eyes half closed.

"Holy cow," she said, peering out of the round door. "What time is it?"

Tommy's mom stepped back another step. She had her hand on Tommy's shoulder trying to pull him back with her. But Tommy was fascinated by this strange little woman who held onto the door as though she might fall down if she let go.

"Eleven. You told me to come up, Twink," his mom said, trying to pull Tommy back. "I thought you meant today."

Twink stared hard at Tommy's mom as though she wasn't sure she'd ever seen her before. Then she looked up at the sky as though she thought maybe his mom was lying about it being eleven o'clock. "I did?"

"Yes. Yesterday in the bar. Remember? I'm Susan Bridges. I came in from the audition . . . and had a drink and . . ."

The word "audition" struck a cord with Twink. "Oh, sure," she said smiling a crumpled smile. "Yeah, sure, honey. I remember. What did you say your name was?"

"Susan Bridges. Say, listen," his mom said, taking a firm hold on Tommy's shoulder and practically yanking him off his feet. "If it's not convenient . . ."

Twink Mondragon reached out as fast as an outfielder stretching for a high ball and grabbed hold of Susan Bridges' arm. "No, no," she said. "Now that you're here you might as well come in. Come on, come on," and she as much as hauled Tommy's mother through the round door into the house. "You, too, kid," she called over her shoulder.

Just to hear the doorbell ring again, Tommy pressed on the bell push as he went in. The trumpets reverberated through the house like an organ in an empty church. If they sounded loud from outside, inside they were deafening. Twink bounced against the wall clutching at her ears.

"Enough, kid," she screamed. "Cut it out!"

The trumpets died away into a distant ringing, leaving behind them a hushed silence. Twink was pale.

"I gotta get that damn door fixed," she croaked. "Hasn't worked since my ex left and I keep meaning to get it fixed. You don't notice it unless you got a head. And I've got a head like Mount Rushmore today," she said, pulling herself together. "Let's be kind to old Twink today, eh, kid?"

"Gee, I'm sorry, Mrs. Mondragon," Tommy said, "But I didn't know . . ."

"Miss," Twink said, leading them into the kitchen. She looked around it like it was a strange room, a room in some other person's house. Dirty dishes were piled high in the sink, cupboards stood open, flour was spilled on the floor. "*Miss* Mondragon," she said. "Mondragon is my professional name. Catches the attention, you know. You've got to catch their attention. Swartz was my married name, but Twink Swartz—it doesn't have it, you know?"

She looked absently around the untidy kitchen, found what she was looking for, and picked it out of the jumble on the counter. She held the electric kettle up to her ear and shook it. Satisfied, she plugged it into a socket be-hind the stove.

"Coffee?" she said.

"Thank you," Susan Bridges said, and from the way she said it Tommy knew she was shocked.

"Got to be instant," Twink Mondragon said, pushing some jars around on the counter.

"That'll be fine."

"How about you, kid?" Twink said. "Ice cream?"

"Sure," Tommy said.

Twink opened the freezer and took out a half-empty quart carton. She pulled out a drawer and took out a spoon. "Here you go," she said, handing him the carton and the spoon. Tommy looked at his mother, who raised her shoulders a little and looked away. He took the carton and started to eat the ice cream out of it.

"You were married?" Susan Bridges asked.

"Married?" said Twink. "I could write the manual. And if I did, the first word I'd write is 'Forget It.' Marriage is the pits, the absolute pits. What about you?"

Now he knew his mom would talk about his dad dying and then meeting Pete and wanting to get married and all that stuff, so he wandered away from the door. The house was kind of interesting, he thought. Interesting and dif-ferent. Twink Mondragon must have a real strange life. She had a pinball machine and a Pachenco machine right in the living room. She had the regular type of furniture, too, but it didn't look as though it got much cleaning. The couch had stains on it and the rug was trampled flat. He went through the door at the end of the living room and found himself in a small den. There were candles set out on a coffee table that was encrusted with wax. Two Siamese cats, white and fawn with crossed eyes, were curled up on the sofa. They looked at him without moving, with their eyes narrowed and their tails curled around them.

Beyond the den was a pool deck. The pool was oblong. Partially submerged, a half-deflated air mattress floated in the water. The deck furniture was beat-up, the umbrella above the round table torn, both the lounge chairs were missing straps. **2004097**

"I know one thing for sure, honey," Twink Mondragon said, leading his mom out onto the deck. "You can't have a career *and* a man, no way." She squinted up at the sun like she could stare it down, but it stayed right where it was, so she pulled a chair into the shade of the torn umbrella. "If I hadn't got married, I coulda been a star. Biggest mistake I ever made." She glared at Susan Bridges as though somehow it might be her fault.

The ice cream was gone from the carton. Tommy scraped his spoon against the bottom. The sound recalled Twink Mondragon to the present.

"Take a swim, kid," she said, swiveling to look at him. "Shuck your duds and get in. Ain't nobody here but us chickens to see you."

"He's got his suit on," Susan Bridges said. "He's got it on under his Levis."

"Suit yourself," Twink said, and laughed at her pun.

Tommy stepped out of his Levis and dove in. He braced himself for the shock of cold water, but when he hit, he got a shock of quite another type. He hit the surface of the water and it was as hot as soup. He sunk into it and came up gasping.

"It's hot," he said.

Twink Mondragon looked over her shoulder. "Solar heat. I got solar heat for the pool. Saves energy."

Now that he was used to it, it wasn't so bad. Tommy struggled to the air mattress and climbed on. He lay there half in and half out of the water, with his legs dragging in the warm pool.

"Only something's wrong with the system," Twink was saying. "One of these days I guess I should get it fixed."

Tommy floated on the old mattress. The sun was high in the sky, burning white, floating over the valley like a huge beach ball.

"You want to be an actress, right?" Twink said.

"Yes, I do," Tommy heard his mom say, and then she said, "I've wanted to be one all my life," which he knew wasn't true. She'd never even mentioned acting until she had the fight with Pete. That was the first Tommy had ever heard about her wanting to be an actress. The day after the fight she'd said they were coming down to Los Angeles so she could take acting lessons. Pete hated Los Angeles. He always said it was a big phony town full of little people all puffed out with air to make them look bigger. That was why his mom had said it. To make Pete mad. And it did. He walked right out of the house. They stayed two more days packing up, but he didn't come back.

That was about the dumbest thing Tommy ever heard anybody say or do, Tommy figured, but his mom had done it and it was too late now. But he couldn't get mad at her. Not anymore. At first when they were down here, he'd been real mad at his mom, as mad as Pete was. He figured that if she just went back up there and said she was sorry, Pete would forget all about the fight. Then one day his mom explained to him that it wasn't just about L.A. The fight was about lots of things, most of all the future. Pete didn't want to be tied down. They'd lived with Pete almost two years and Tommy wanted it to last forever and his mom did, but Pete . . . Pete just wanted to go along day by day and not think about the future, not the real long, long future. And Tommy's mom figured that if that's the way he felt, well, Pete didn't love her, and if he didn't love her, then she'd better leave now.

She got a job right off when they came down to L.A., working at the answering service. That way she could go to acting classes in the day and, who knows, maybe she could be an actress just as she said she would be. She saw lots of women on television who weren't any better than she was, she was sure of it, so why not?

So here they were, down in L.A., and Pete was up north by himself.

"I can tell you one thing, honey," Twink Mondragon's voice said, "in this town it isn't *what* you know that counts. It's *who* you know."

Tommy tuned out. He floated on the limp air mattress and thought about his new friend Joel who'd run away from home and who lived by himself in the deserted estate. Well, not quite by himself. There was the Indian, of course, but Tommy hadn't seen him . . . *yet.*

6

"YOUR MOM SOUNDS like a flake," Joel said.

"She is not!"

"Well, this Twink character. *She's* a flake."

"Yeah, Twink's a flake all right," Tommy agreed.

They were lying on a ledge on the canyon wall. Below them in a clearing stood the teepee where the Indian lived. The Indian had covered a framework of three long poles with dead palm fronds to make the teepee.

"You think he's going to come out?"

"If he's in there," Joel said. "He gets up pretty early sometimes. He might be out hunting rabbits. That's what he lives on. Lots of rabbits in the canyon. The snakes eat 'em."

Tommy stared down the hillside at the teepee. He couldn't see any sign of life down there. But he couldn't hear anything either. He couldn't hear anybody moving around in the brush. He couldn't see any bushes move or any birds fly out of the trees.

"He's an Indian," Joel said when Tommy told him that he didn't think anybody could be hunting since nothing was moving down below. "Indians can move without making any noise."

"In the olden days . . ." Tommy began, speaking more loudly than he had intended.

"Shut up," Joel ordered him. "You'll warn him!"

"If he's there!" Tommy said in the same voice. He was mad at Joel for ordering him around.

"I *told* you to be quiet," Joel whispered.

"Well, if you'd *ask* once in a while instead of just ordering everyone around, I'd do it."

Joel scowled. Tommy didn't mean to get Joel mad, but sometimes Joel was just plain rude. It seemed strange to Tommy that a boy who came from a rich home in Beverly Hills would have such bad manners, but then it seemed strange to Tommy that anyone could run away from a nice home. Joel was strange, period, Tommy decided, but that didn't make him any less a friend. "You don't choose your friends," Pete used to say. "They happen. And you don't try to change them, either."

"I'm sorry," Tommy said, thinking about what Pete would say at his correcting Joel.

"That's all garbage," Joel said, still scowling.

Tommy dropped the subject. The bushes had yellow flowers on them. The canyon wall was patched like a country quilt, yellow and different shades of green and some purple and scarlet blossoms where the bougainvillaea grew. Tommy felt good. He didn't really care whether they saw the Indian. He just liked being with Joel. He liked it a lot better than being up at Twink's pool.

"She had cats," Tommy said. "Two Siamese cats with mean eyes, skinny cats."

"Some people like cats, some like dogs," Joel said. "Now, dogs, they like people, but cats, they like places. A dog won't mind if you move away, so long as you take him with you, but a cat, he'd just as soon stay behind and let you go."

"Pete liked dogs," Tommy said.

"Kinda figured he would," Joel said with a laugh. "You're real hung up on that Pete guy."

Tommy rolled on his back and looked up at the sky through the branches of the trees. "Pete was like a dad," he said, something he'd never said to anyone.

After a while Joel said, "Well, I can tell you that not all dads are terrific. Some . . . they're real turkeys. A kid's better off with no father than with a turkey."

Tommy couldn't buy that. When he looked at other kids riding to the hardware store on Saturdays with their fathers, when he saw them in restaurants, when their fathers came to school, he knew that that's what he wanted most in the world. He didn't want to live in a big house, he didn't want bicycles or pools or any of that. What he wanted was a father he could talk to.

He lay on his stomach watching the teepee and said so, and as he spoke he could see Joel getting madder and madder. But he didn't care. Joel could think what he wanted.

Tommy wasn't going to sit here and listen to stuff like what Joel was saying. Tommy knew—he *knew*—that the best thing a boy could have was a guy to help him along, a guy like Pete who listened when Tommy talked and didn't laugh at him when he asked a stupid question.

"I think you're stupid to run away from your dad," he said recklessly when he had finished talking. "If I could have stayed with Pete, I'd have stayed forever. But Pete wasn't my dad and I couldn't. Running away from home's real stupid."

Joel's face was as red as a tomato. His eyes were blazing. He was breathing fast. He stood up and started to unbutton his shirt. Tommy thought maybe Joel was going to take his shirt off and beat him up. But he wasn't moving. He'd said what he wanted to say and he was going to stand and stick it out, no matter what Joel started. Pete always said a guy didn't have to go looking for a fight, but when he had one on his hands he might as well stick it out.

Joel was so mad he could hardly get the shirt off. The last two buttons tore away. He stripped the shirt off, ripping one of the sleeves as he peeled it down his arm, and then he turned his back on Tommy and yelled, "So you think all dads are terrific, do you? What about that? That's what my old man did to me."

And Tommy saw that all across Joel's back were welt marks made by a strap.

The sight of the strap marks hit Tommy as though it was him who had been beaten. He couldn't speak right away.

"Kids like you make me sick," Joel said, his hands

shaking as he put his shirt back on again. "You're always whining. 'Poor me. I don't have a father.' You don't know when you're well off. I've got a father and I wish to hell he'd fall off a roof and knock his brains out. Maybe then we'd get some peace at home."

"I'm sorry," Tommy whispered. "I'm sorry, Joel."

"Now you are, now that you've got everybody whipped up," Joel said, pulling the torn sleeve away from the shirt. One bare arm showed, tanned brown. He did up the buttons that were still on the shirt. "When we lived with Pete! When we lived with Pete! I don't even live with you and I'm sick of hearing about Pete. Wouldn't blame your mom if she ran away herself, hearing about Pete all day long."

He looked like a tattered scarecrow standing there in his torn shirt. "Look at me. I can't go down the boulevard now. The cops'll pick me up sure."

"I'll get you a new shirt," Tommy said.

"Where are you going to get me a shirt?" Joel demanded. "Your shirts are too small for me. I suppose you got one of Pete's shirts hidden under your mattress or something, like a good luck charm."

"You shut up about Pete," Tommy said. "You don't know him."

"Sounds like a selfish son-of-a-gun to me," Joel said, trying to see if the sleeve could be sewn back on. He wasn't looking when Tommy knocked him down. "What the hell you think you're doing?" Joel yelled as they rolled over into the brush, but Tommy was hitting him as hard as he could with his fists, hitting him for what he said about Pete and all the other things that had made Tommy mad. Joel tried to hold him off at first, saying, "Whoa now, kid, whoa now, boy. You don't know what you're asking for," but Tommy wouldn't stop. The more he hit Joel the angrier he got for lots of reasons, not all of them to do with what Joel had said about Pete. Tommy was angry, really angry, angrier than he had known he was. "All right," Joel warned him as they tumbled down the hillside, "you asked for it." And he grabbed Tommy by the throat in a hard grip, hauled back and belted him such a blow that Tommy's head rung like a siren, his eyes crossed, and then he felt nothing, nothing at all except a feeling that he was falling down, down, down. Then he must have passed out for a little while, for he didn't feel anything, and the next thing he knew everything was very, very quiet, the siren in his head had stopped, and he heard the gentle sounds of the hot wind in the canyon and, in the distance, the rat-a-tat-tat of a woodpecker drilling a tree.

He opened his eyes and found himself face down in the dust, with dirt in his mouth and his face scratched from the fall. He sat up and wanted to be sick, so he had to bend over, and he sat there with his legs stretched out and his head bent down between his knees until the feeling passed. Then he sat up trying to figure out where he was.

The first thing he saw clearly was the palm leaves of the Indian's teepee. His heart took a jolt. He was sitting in the dirt about two feet away from the teepee's opening. He could see inside where there was a blanket and some pots. The teepee was empty, but while he was staring in there he got the feeling that he was not alone. The hairs on the back of his neck prickled like a dog that senses trouble and he turned his head very slowly to look behind him.

The Indian was standing in the shade of the trees. He wore long leather pants with a fringe down the seam on each side. His faded cotton shirt was open to show a bare chest tanned a dark wood-brown, and his black hair was pulled back with a leather thong. But it wasn't his clothes that Tommy saw most clearly. What he saw was the Indian's eyes. They were jet black, narrowed to slits, and full of fury.

7

THE INDIAN STEPPED into the clearing, reached down, and pulled Tommy to his feet. He shook Tommy hard, setting his head ringing like a school bell.

"Hey," Tommy cried. "That hurts."

The Indian glared at him. His eyes glazed with anger. He opened his mouth and said, "You're about the dumbest kid I ever saw."

Tommy stared at him in surprise. "You speak English!"

"You were expecting maybe Italian?" he said. "I lived in this country all my life. Sure I speak English."

Tommy's head hurt. "I got a headache," he said.

"Serves you right," the Indian said, releasing Tommy's arm. There were red marks where the Indian's fingers had been. He was one strong guy, that Indian. But he wasn't very big, maybe five foot nine or ten. He'd looked big standing under the tree with his eyes narrowed with anger. "Don't you know there's snakes in that brush?"

Tommy looked back up the hillside. There wasn't any sign of Joel. The bushes still vibrated very slightly.

"And you," the Indian yelled up the hill. "The other one, come on down here before you get in trouble."

Far up the side of the canyon the bushes moved, the little yellow flowers jiggling on their stems.

"Yeah, you!" the Indian called. "Get down here!"

Joel came out from behind the bush and started down to the canyon floor.

"Take it easy, too," the Indian said. "There are rattle-snakes up there."

Joel said, "Ain't but two types of rattlers that are killers. One is the Mojave green that you find in the north of the State. The other's the sidewinder. That's in the desert. These here rattlers, they won't kill you!"

The little Indian turned on his heel and went into the teepee. He came out with a book in his hand. "What's that?" he demanded, showing a picture to Joel.

"That's a rattler, all right," Joel said. "It'd make you sick as hell if he took a swipe at you. Wouldn't kill you!"

The Indian showed the cover to the two boys indignantly. "What's that say? What's that say!"

Tommy read it. "Poisonous Snakes of the West."

"Right!" the Indian said triumphantly. " 'Poisonous Snakes of the West.' Well, I'm telling you I saw one of those right up there."

Joel looked unconvinced. "Didn't say it wasn't poisonous," he said. "I said it wouldn't kill you. Might kill a little runt like Tommy, but wouldn't kill me. Wouldn't kill you. What's an Indian need with a book like that, anyway?"

The Indian looked abashed. He closed the book quickly. "My name's Little Horse," he said defiantly.

Tommy was still mad at Joel, madder now at being called a runt. "What do you know about rattlesnakes?" he asked. "You live in Beverly Hills, don't you?"

The Indian saw his chance. "Mr. Beverly Hills," he said. "Mr. Know It All!" He took the book back inside his teepee and came out with a first-aid kit. "You look like hell," he said to Tommy, and unpacked a bottle of iodine and some cotton.

Tommy backed away.

"Listen," said the Indian, advancing on him. "That cut will get infected." He opened the bottle and dabbed at Tommy's scraped head with the cotton soaked in iodine. Tommy kept his eyes shut tight and didn't squeal. Joel watched while the Indian cleaned the wound.

"Thought you Indians crushed some berries for that stuff," Joel said. "Never heard of an Indian with a first-aid kit. What type of an Indian are you?"

"Don't listen to him," Tommy said, because he could tell the Indian was hurt. "He's mad because I tore his shirt. I'll get you a new shirt," he said to Joel.

"Oh, sure," said Joel.

"I will!"

"Where are you going to get the money? Steal it?"

"I get an allowance Friday," Tommy said, while the Indian dabbed at his scratches with iodine. "Ow, that hurts."

"Friday. Three days. If I go down the boulevard like this, the cops'll bust me. How'm I going to live for three days up here? Have to live on berries like the Indian."

Little Horse tightened the top of the iodine bottle and put it back in the first-aid kit. "Why the cops want you?"

"None of your business."

Tommy was getting mad at Joel again. He was getting mad now because Joel was being rude to Little Horse. "He's a runaway," he said. Little Horse said nothing. He went back inside the teepee and came out with a needle and thread. "Gimme your shirt," he said to Joel, "and one word more and I'll bust you one in the mouth."

Joel looked at the needle and thread and he looked at Little Horse, but he thought twice about laughing. Instead he took off his shirt and handed it over with the torn sleeve.

He kept his back turned to hide the welts.

Tommy asked, "How long have you lived here?"

"Couple of months," Little Horse replied, sitting down on a rock with the two pieces of the shirt on his lap. He licked the thread and held the needle up to the light to thread it. After several unsuccessful tries he said, "Would you go in there and get my glasses? The old eyes aren't what they used to be."

"Your glasses!" said Joel.

But Little Horse just stared hard at Joel, and instead of making fun of him, Joel did what he was told. He went into the teepee. To do so he had to turn his back, and then Little Horse saw the red marks across his back. He didn't say anything right off but he looked from Joel's back to Tommy, who sat with his lips pressed hard together, hoping the Indian wouldn't ask him about Joel's back. That was Joel's business. But Little Horse looked away up at the tree tops and the ridge around the canyon, and the creases in his face got deeper. He was thinking.

Joel didn't come out with the glasses. He came out holding a striped suit on a hanger. "What's this?"

"What's it look like?" said Little Horse. "It's a suit." He didn't speak angrily. The sight of Joel's back seemed to have made him sad.

"What's an Indian need a suit for?" Joel asked, holding the suit on its hanger high, at arm's length, as though he were selling it.

The Indian paused before he answered, looking the boy over for a few seconds, and then he said quietly, "I need it Thursdays to do down to the Unemployment Office."

Something about the way he spoke stopped Joel from what he was going to do, laugh. Instead he stood there with the suit still held high, looking foolish, then he lowered it and went back in the teepee and got the glasses.

The Indian sat quietly sewing the sleeve back on the shirt while Joel walked around the small clearing. The afternoon was very quiet. Some noises came from in the brush, birds shuffling among the dead leaves, the sudden movement of a small animal setting the bushes shaking for a moment.

"Where you get your water?" Joel asked.

"Over there. There's a tap." The Indian waved the needle with its length of blue thread attached to the shirt.

Joel went where he gestured and said, "You've let it run off."

"Right," the Indian said. "Why not?"

"The ground's all wet."

"So?"

"So that's what brings the snakes," said Joel. "Right now when it's all dry, they look for water. They like to lie where it's damp and get the water through their skin." He started kicking dirt over the wet earth. "You got a rope?" he asked.

"No."

"You should get one. Stretch a rough rope around the teepee and no snake will cross it. Bet you don't sleep much at night, thinking 'bout those snakes."

The Indian broke the thread with his teeth. "Where you run away from?" he asked.

"Beverly Hills," Joel said quickly.

The Indian held the shirt out to him. "Where?" he asked.

"Beverly Hills!" Joel said again loudly, reaching for the shirt. The Indian didn't let it go right away. He held it and looked at Joel for a long moment as though maybe he didn't believe him, and Joel flushed. "Beverly Hills," Joel repeated, jerking the shirt out of the Indian's hand. "Where you from?"

"New York City," said the Indian.

"New York City!" said Joel. "New York City! That's

the damnedest thing I ever heard. An Indian from New York City."

"You think there are no Indians in New York City?" said Little Horse. "Who you think sold Manhattan to the Dutch? The Indians, that's who, Mr. Beverly Hills."

Joel was putting his shirt on. "An Indian from New York City," he chuckled. "With a suit for the unemployment line." He stopped with the shirt half on and half off. "Come on, tell me the truth, what are you really? You're not Indian. I know Indians. Man, I've seen Indians all my life. Back home . . ." He stopped and again he flushed, turning his back and putting on his shirt hurriedly.

"Back home in Beverly Hills?" asked the Indian. "That what you were going to say?"

"You oughta get a rope," Joel said, buttoning up his shirt. "The snakes don't like the rough feel. They won't cross it so long as you keep it clear. Shake it out every day, every night, and you can sleep safe. Safe as you would be back in Man-hattan, Big Chief Little Horse. Safer, maybe."

Little Horse stood up and asked, "You boys hungry?"

That got Joel's attention. "What you got?"

"This ain't a diner," Little Horse said. "You take what you get and be glad of it. I'm not feeding any kid who lips me off, either. Got it?"

Joel turned away scowling. The Indian watched him for a minute, and then went into his teepee. He came out with a saucepan, a package of hot dogs, and two cans of beans.

"Beans and franks," he said. "How's that sound?"

"Great," Tommy said.

But Joel was still sulking. "Don't sound Indian to me," he said. "Thought maybe we'd have deer or pemmican or something." But he didn't say it to Little Horse. Joel spoke with his back turned, so he was facing the trees. He was still facing that way when Little Horse kicked him hard in the butt, knocking him on his face in the dirt. Tommy was so surprised he leaped up as if he were the one who'd been kicked, but he wasn't as surprised as Joel. Joel spun around as fast as a snake himself, his face streaked with dirt, and he came up mean, mean and angry.

"You," he said, pointing at the Indian while he wiped dirt out of his mouth. "You're gonna be real sorry, Mr. Manhattan Indian, that you did that," and he circled away from Little Horse, kind of bent over like a wrestler. "I'm gonna kick the Manhattan pants offa you for doing that."

Little Horse stayed right where he was, but he turned as Joel turned, never letting Joel have his back. He threw the saucepan and the package of hot dogs out of the way and said to Tommy out of the side of his mouth, "Here, catch," and then he tossed the two cans of beans to Tommy, who caught them awkwardly. Then he took his time taking off his shirt, still keeping Joel in front of him. When Little Horse had his shirt off, Tommy thought maybe Joel had real trouble on his hands. Little Horse was short but he was tough. He had muscles on muscles, a solid body and a broad chest, and down his stomach the muscles were lined up like stepping stones.

Watching each other carefully, they circled slowly, slowly around the clearing. The Indian jumped forward, hit Joel hard with his fist on the shoulder, and jumped back as the boy staggered to keep his balance.

"Come on, come on, Mr. Beverly Hills, let's see it."

Joel's eyes narrowed. He crouched, lunged forward to the left, but as the Indian turned left, Joel changed direction fast as lightning, hitting him above the waist. The Indian doubled up, spun around, looked like he was going down, but stood up quickly, one leg out to trip the boy.

"Dirty fighter, eh," he said. "Street fighting. You didn't learn that in no snooty neighborhood." The leg caught Joel behind the knees and he went over backward.

The Indian threw himself down at the boy, but Joel crawled away like a crab, leaving the Indian to land on his face in the dirt. Joel jumped him, hammering away at the Indian's head. Little Horse took it for a few seconds, winded from his fall, but then the muscles in his bare back flexed, swelling up huge, and in one move he threw Joel off him, right across the clearing at the teepee. Joel hit the teepee in midair, falling down into the ruins of palm fronds, the unemployment suit, and cans of food that rolled out into the dirt. The Indian waded in through all the mess, grabbed the boy by his ankles and hauled him out into the open. Joel lay there in the grass face down, panting, the welts from his earlier beating bright red across his back.

"Now," said Little Horse. "Where you come from?"

Joel lay there not answering, his back going up and down as he gasped for each breath.

"I asked you where you came from, kid," the Indian said. "You ain't no Beverly Hills brat."

(53)

Still Joel didn't answer. Little Horse leaned down and grabbed one of the boy's arms, twisting it behind him. The boy rolled over, crying out in pain.

"Where you from?" the Indian demanded.

"Idaho!" Joel cried. "Idaho! Idaho. Klamath Falls, Idaho!"

The Indian dropped Joel's arm. He wasn't mad anymore. He looked sad, ashamed of himself. He reached down to help Joel up. "Leave me alone," Joel said. "You dumb twit! Leave me alone."

Tommy held his breath, thinking the Indian would hit Joel again for that. But Little Horse just stood over Joel, looking down on him, and then Tommy saw that Joel wasn't panting for breath anymore. The heaving of his back was Joel crying, crying quietly into the dirt, keeping his face down so no one could see his tears.

Little Horse looked at Tommy helplessly. Tommy could see that he felt terrible, that he wanted to help Joel, but he didn't know what to say.

"Joel . . ." Tommy said.

"Go to hell," Joel said. "Get lost."

The Indian sighed. The trees waved in the hot afternoon air, moving shadows across the clearing with the destroyed teepee in the center, the suit, the food, all the mess of the fight all about, and the short sweating figure of the Indian standing over the boy in the dirt.

"Listen, kid," Little Horse said quietly. "I ain't no Wild West Indian. I'm a fake too. Me . . . I'm a cab driver from New York City."

Nobody moved. Tommy looked at Little Horse. He

still looked like an Indian to him, with the clothes and the teepee and all that stuff. But the only Indians Tommy had ever seen had been on television.

Joel was breathing evenly. Without raising his head he said, "You're still a twit."

8

JUST A FEW minutes had gone by since Joel and Little Horse had begun to fight, but it seemed to Tommy that hours had passed. Little Horse began to pick up the cans that had rolled out of the teepee. Joel lay where he was, panting. Tommy helped Little Horse clean up.

They worked silently, stacking the canned goods on one side of the clearing. Little Horse shook out his unemployment suit and hung it on the branch of a tree.

Joel got up while they worked and wandered out of the clearing. Little Horse stopped for a few seconds, watching Joel as he threaded his way through the bushes, but then Little Horse went back to the job he was doing. When Joel came back he looked better. His face was clean. He had some more scratches that he hadn't had before and if you looked closely you could see he'd been crying because his eyes were puffy.

He stood in the middle of the clearing, looking around. "You had it all wrong anyway," he said quietly.

Little Horse watched him warily.

"This where you been cooking?" Joel asked, pointing out a ring of stones with ashes in the middle.

Little Horse nodded. Tommy finished stacking up the cans. A couple of them had lost their labels.

Joel ran his hand over his head, pushing his hair back. "Wind's all wrong here," he said. "Get a Santa Ana some- day and the wind'll blow the sparks right into the teepee, set the whole place on fire." He waved at the canyon all about. "Everything, maybe. Burn you like a barbecue. No way could you get out of here."

He kicked the palm fronds with the toe of his boot. "Wind'll blow these away anyway, right? Bet you lose a couple every night, right?"

Little Horse nodded. "Doesn't bother me," he said. "Nights are warm."

"Now they are," Joel said. "Come December, it'll be as cold as hell. People think California's hot all year. It ain't. Winter nights get cold in California!"

"How do you know that?" asked Little Horse. "You're from Idaho!"

Joel glanced at him to see what he meant by that. Little Horse held the boy's glance until Joel turned away again and looked at Tommy, who was watching both of them closely. "Country boys got more sense than you city folk," Joel said. "We find things out ahead of time. We don't wait for one cold night to freeze our butts solid before we know California has winter too. I was fixing to move on November sometime, earlier maybe. Try Florida. Now Florida, that's different," he said with the ghost of a smile. "You 'Indians' can set your teepees up anywhere in Forida. Most all of Florida is warm all year, what I hear."

Little Horse's mouth twisted reluctantly into a smile. "You hear that, eh?"

"That's what I hear," Joel repeated.

Nobody said anything for a couple of minutes, but Tommy could see that Joel and Little Horse were friends now somehow. To break the silence he said, "When we lived with Pete, it got real cold in the winter. Course, we lived on the beach. We got the breeze off the Santa Barbara Channel."

"You ain't heard about Pete yet," Joel said sideways to Little Horse with a smile. "Pete's sorta like the Big Chief of the Pacific Coast, what I hear. Ain't nobody like Pete."

"I didn't say that!" Tommy said.

"Pete, now, he wouldn't do any damn fool thing like build a teepee in the bottom of a canyon. Pete, he'd build it some place nice and safe like."

"Listen," Tommy warned, "you shut up about Pete."

Joel turned his back on Tommy. Tommy said to Little Horse, "Pete was this guy my mom and I lived with. He's an abalone diver."

"Sort of like an Indian from Manhattan," Joel said.

"Shut up!" Tommy warned him.

"You're really asking to get your butt busted, man," Little Horse said to Joel. "You don't like anybody, do you? And you make real sure nobody will like you."

Joel flushed. "I don't care 'bout that," he said. "I like you, you like me, all that stuff. That's all a crock." He spoke kind of sadly, though.

"I liked Pete," Tommy said. "And Pete liked me."

"Sure he did," Little Horse said, patting Tommy on the shoulder before Joel could say anything. "Don't listen to sour-mug over there. You listen to him, you'll end up like him."

Surprisingly Tommy suddenly felt sorry for Joel. "He doesn't mean it," he said. He thought of the marks on Joel's back and the lies he'd told him. "Joel's my friend, too," he said. "Pete used to say . . ." and he stopped to see if Joel was going to make a joke again, but Joel wasn't. He was listening to Tommy with a strange look on his face. "Pete used to say," Tommy said again, "that some of the best friends you have aren't always the ones who talk about being friends all the time. A friend is a guy who treats you right, not just a guy who says he's your friend."

"Treats you right like throwing you down the hill?" Joel said, breaking out that big, knockdown smile he could flash when he wanted.

"Pete sounds like quite a guy," Little Horse said. "I guess you miss him."

Tommy didn't want to talk about missing Pete. He missed Pete so bad sometimes, he thought he could really feel the pain. Thinking about it made it worse.

"Where would you put the teepee, Joel?" he asked, to change the subject.

Joel jerked his hand up to the head of the canyon. "Up there."

They followed the direction of his arm. High up on the rim of the canyon was the elegant form of the small gazebo etched against the afternoon sky.

"Way up there?" Little Horse said. "That's a hell of a distance from the gate."

"Yeah, but you'd be safe from fire," Joel said. "Down here, one mistake, you'll be burned to a crisp." He laughed mercilessly. "You and the rest of us, we get caught without warning."

"What rest?"

"Me," Joel said. "Ain't that enough?"

Little Horse looked up at the distant shell of the gazebo. He was thinking. Finally he said, "Why don't you live up there?"

"I don't cook," Joel said. "No danger of fire where I am if I don't cook. Besides," he said, "I got other things to worry about."

"Like what?"

"The crazies."

The way Little Horse stared at Joel, Tommy thought maybe he wasn't going to ask who the crazies were. Little Horse stared at Joel a long time, but then he said, "Who crazies?"

"Down the boulevard," Joel said.

"They're real strange," Tommy said, because he felt he was being left out. "Joel took me down there. Most of them are runaways and they've got to stay out of the way of the cops. They look sick, some of them." As he spoke he realized that Joel was a runaway, too, not just from Beverly Hills, across town, but from way up in Idaho. He'd always figured Joel could just hop a bus and go home any time he got tired of the estate, but Idaho, that was a long way. He looked at Joel to see if he looked any different now that he knew he wasn't a rich kid runaway, but just a regular kid from Idaho, but Joel looked just the same. He was standing there in the sunlight telling Little Horse how things were just the way he told Tommy what was what.

"You afraid of those guys?" Little Horse asked Joel.

Joel laughed kind of funny. "Afraid?" he said. "Sure I'm afraid. Man, I tell you, what some of those dudes shoot in them, you have to be crazy yourself not to be afraid of them. Don't tell me no big-time 'Manhattan Indian' ain't smart enough to be afraid of the street kids. The street kids, they're real dangerous. They ain't got nothing to lose." He flung his arm in the direction of the hillside. "Those rattlers out there, they hit on you, it's because they're scared. You get too close to the nest, they hit you. Most the time, you stay away, they leave you alone. They don't want any more to do with you than you want with them. But those dudes down there," and he flung his arm this time in the direction of Hollywood Boulevard, "they hit on you just for the fun of it, you know. They ain't got nothing and they know it. They get a chance to kick a little tail themselves 'stead of getting their own tail kicked, they gonna take it. Man, I stay out of their way. I see them coming, I get scarce."

Little Horse said, "So O.K. I hear you." He looked back up the canyon. "That's one hell of a long way to haul things."

Joel pushed one of the cans that had rolled away from

the stack with his foot. "We'll help you, won't we, Tommy?"

"Sure," Tommy said. "That's not so far."

"Listen to him," Joel scoffed, but nicely this time. " 'That's not so far.' That's one hell of a distance, kid," he said, "but if we get Mr. Manhattan up there maybe I can sleep safe, so up there we go. Right?"

"Right," said Tommy.

They both looked at Little Horse.

He shrugged. "Who am I to argue? I'm just a dumb cab driver from New York City."

9

Working together, they got all of Little Horse's belongings up to the top of the canyon. They got his canned goods, his book on how to live off the wild berries, his snake book, his first-aid kit, his pots and pans, and his unemployment suit. The haul took them two hours, and at the end of it they were exhausted. The three of them lay on the ground in the shade of the gazebo, completely wiped out.

"So now we're up here," Little Horse said. "What happens now?"

Above them the gazebo was in pretty good shape. It had a roof, the pillars were firm, it had a little balcony that ran all around it, and at one side a flight of six wide steps led up from the ground to the flat, smooth floor of the little garden house. They were right at the crest of the

Hollywood Hills here. Over the hill to the right was the San Fernando Valley, stretching off as flat as a mesa, criss-crossed with the freeways, with Universal Studios visible in the distance, bright as a silver dollar in the sunshine. Straight ahead like a miniature city was downtown Los Angeles, and down to the right beyond the canyon was Hollywood, with the round Capitol Records building and the strange shape of the Magic Castle on its own little hill.

Right ahead of them, just below the gazebo, was a hole in the ground about a hundred yards long, like a swimming pool, except this wasn't any swimming pool. This had once been the basement of a house, a large house. The walls were gone but some of the windows were still framed against the sky, empty of glass, just the wooden frames and, hanging from them, the torn remnants of curtains, ghostly as they blew in the breeze that came right in from the ocean across all that smog to this, the highest point in the Hollywood Hills.

"Will you look at that," Joel said. "That must have been some house once. I don't think I've ever seen a house as big as that, not built, that is. I've seen pictures of houses off in Europe, places like that, houses for kings and such stuff, but I ain't ever seen one close up. Wish I'd seen this one 'fore it tumbled down."

"What happened to it?" Tommy asked.

"Looks like fire to me," Little Horse said. "See, all the wood is charred."

No one said anything for quite a while. They lay in the shade of the gazebo looking at the ruins of the house, dreaming what it must have looked like once upon a time when it was new. Joel got up eventually and clomped up the steps to the gazebo and stood looking around in every direction.

"Man would feel like a king living up here," he said. "On a clear day I bet I could see back to Idaho from up here." He turned around further. "I can see right out to Beverly Hills from here. Hey, further even. I can see the ocean!"

"Where?" Tommy called, scrambling up onto the platform. "Let me see." He stood beside Joel, looking in the same direction. He could see the rolling hills of Beverly Hills with Sunset Strip winding along at the foot, with tiny little cars like toys, creeping along. "Where's the ocean?"

Joel looked at him disgustedly. "You're too short," he said, and when Tommy stood as straight as he could and still couldn't see the ocean, Joel said, "Here," and lifted him up onto the rail. Tommy strained his eyes looking for waves like there'd been outside Pete's cabin on the beach, but all he could see was what looked like the sky and, low down, some clouds.

"I don't see it."

"There!" Joel said, holding onto him with one hand and pointing with the other. "See, that white line real low that looks like a cloud. That's the beach. Then just above that, where the sky looks dark, that's not the sky at all, that's the water. That's the ocean. From up here it all looks the same unless you look real close."

Now that Joel pointed it out to him Tommy could see the shoreline and then the dark water of the Pacific and even the line of the horizon where the ocean met the sky.

"I don't remember it like that," he said softly. "When we lived . . ." but he stopped himself.

Joel didn't laugh at him this time. "When you lived with Pete," he said. "You saw it all close up. Things look different when you see them close up. Now here, this is how a rich man sees the ocean, kid. You see the difference?"

"I liked it better close up," Tommy said.

Joel lifted him down. "Difference is," Joel said, "a rich man lives up here and can go *down* there. Now a poor man, he's down there and he can't come up here 'less he's *invited*."

"We're here," Tommy said.

"That's because the rich man ain't home," Joel said. "If he was home, you and me'd be back down there."

Little Horse, who had been listening to all this, said, "Yeah, and rich men have got cars to haul them up and down. That's one heck of a walk for a city boy."

"I think maybe we can work out something, a little track up and down the canyon," Joel said. "A shortcut, like."

"Still a hell of a distance," Little Horse said.

"If we put in some ropes," Joel said, "we could haul anything up here."

"We?"

Joel looked around. "I kinda like it up here," he said. "Feels rich, you know, all that city spread out like a great big toy all about. Thought I might stay up here too."

Little Horse didn't say yes and he didn't say no. He looked around as though he were seeing if there was enough room. Then he looked at Joel for a while. Joel just stared off at the city down below and then out at the horizon. Tommy knew that he was waiting for Little Horse to make up his mind.

"Sure, O.K.," Little Horse said eventually. "But right now I figure we all need something to eat."

Tommy and Joel set out a ring of stones for the fire. Little Horse went off to the ruins of the big house looking for water outlets. He found one and came back hauling a bucket. "Think maybe we could make a small pool out there," he said. "Like a pond or something. Can't figure why they never shut off the water. If we don't use too much, they won't notice. Bet no one's been up here to read a meter in twenty years. 'Mount we use, they'll think it's just a broken pipe, leak, something like that."

They put a pot on the fire when it was ready, heated up the beans and franks, and sat cross-legged on watch above the city, eating out of tin cans. Those beans and franks tasted like the best food Tommy had ever eaten, as good as the fish Pete brought home some nights that he'd caught himself.

The afternoon was late now. They sat there, all three of them in a row, and watched the sun set in the west. It was a terrific sunset, orange mostly and some pink that covered the whole sky like spilled paint.

"Damnedest thing, you know," Joel said after no one had spoken for a long time. "Up where I come from, there's no smog, nothing like the garbage in the air down here. Now, up there, we get sunsets, real nice sunsets, kinda gold and all, but nothin' like this. This now, this is

Technicolor, and you know why? Because there's all that garbage in the air from the cars. The sunlight goes through that and it's like a rainbow. Ain't that the damnedest thing?"

When it came time for Tommy to go home, he felt lonely, left out, sort of, to be leaving Joel and Little Horse up there. He said good-by and they watched him as he trudged off down the first part of the long winding road along the side of the canyon that would take him back to the gates. He looked back a couple of times, and they were still watching. Then it started to get dark real quick, and he got scared, so he began to run. That was a long road, and it wound back and forth all the way down. By the time he got down he was breathing heavily, and the night was almost upon the city. He stood by the gate and looked up, way up to where he knew Joel and Little Horse were, but he couldn't see anything. It was all dark up there, the canyon blacker with shadow than the sky. Above the rim the stars were coming out, and a jet was coming in far up in the night sky, the lights on the wings winking red and green. He stood and strained his eyes looking for some sign of the gazebo. The night was too dark and it was getting late. He crawled through the gate and out into the city. Lights had come on all over and the noise seemed louder, as the city wound up for the night. He walked home quickly.

10

"MY GOD, WHERE have you *been?*" His mother took him by the shoulders and held him at arm's length. She pulled him in to kiss him and pushed him out again to look at him. "Where did those bruises come from? I've been half out of my mind with worry!"

"I was with friends."

"Who?"

"Just friends."

She looked at him for a few seconds. He knew that look. She was deciding if he was telling the truth. She was angry.

"You frightened me half to death," she said. "It's dark out, Tommy. This isn't Santa Barbara. You can't wander around alone in the city at night."

"I told you, I *wasn't* alone."

"Where were you?"

"Up in the estate."

"What estate?" she asked quietly. He knew right off he'd made a mistake.

"What's for dinner?" he asked, pulling away.

"What estate, Tommy?"

"The old one at the end of the street."

His mother looked horrified. "You've been up in there? There's a sign on the gate, not to go in."

"Lots of people go in," Tommy said, trying to look cool. "It's just like a park in there."

"Oh, no, it's not," his mother said, moving fast toward him. "There's no police to protect you in there, for one thing."

"Aw, Mom," he said. "I'm not a baby."

"You're my baby," she said.

"Aw, Mom," he repeated, embarrassed.

"Well, you are," she said. "Awful things could happen to you in there and no one would hear you if you called. Terrible things." He could see she was frightening herself all over again and he knew what was coming next if she did. He was right. Next, she said, "Tommy, you make me so mad I could . . . I could . . ." She wanted to say she could spank him, but he was getting too big for that. Pete had walloped him the last time he needed it. That time Tommy had told his mom to butt out of his life, to let him alone, and when she tried to catch him he ran away, a lot faster than she could run. But when he came home, Pete was waiting, and he knew there wasn't any use trying to run from Pete. So he let himself be walloped by Pete and it hurt like the devil. So she couldn't spank him. He knew that. But he also felt kind of sorry for his mom because he was growing up and she could see him growing up right in front of her. He wasn't a little boy any longer, he wasn't her baby, no matter what she said, and for some reason that frightened her. He didn't know why it did, but he knew it did.

She started to cry. Her face screwed up and she tried to hide it by raising her hands, and then she sat down, bent over, and sobbed. He felt awful and went over to put his arm around her. She sobbed away real hard, not letting him look at her, and he knew she wasn't trying to make him feel bad. She couldn't help herself.

The sobs went on for a long time. She sounded like a little kid, a real little kid. Tommy hugged her and leaned over her and kissed her on the back of the neck until she quieted down.

"You're all . . . I've . . . got," she cried. "If anything happened to you, Tommy, I don't know . . . I don't know . . . what I'd do."

When she talked like that he felt worse. He knew how she felt. When he was alone in bed at night, not every night, but some nights, he thought about what it would be like if his mom died. With his dad already dead, he'd be an orphan. There wasn't anyone left. He'd have to go to an orphanage. He didn't know what an orphanage would be like, but when he thought about it, it scared him. He got lonesome, terribly lonesome, and his breath caught in his throat. He'd lie very still until he could breathe properly, and sometimes he'd come out of the bedroom to ask for a glass of milk just to see that his mom was there.

So he knew how she felt, how frightened she was, when she talked like that, and he knew why she cried.

A loud rapping at the door startled both of them. His mother sat up drying her eyes. She made to rise and cross the room to answer the knocking, but before she could the door was flung back to reveal Twink Mondragon.

"You found him!" she said dramatically.

Tommy felt betrayed. If he was late, he was sorry. But he didn't like his mom telling other people about their troubles. He scowled and turned away to go into the bedroom.

"Where was he?" Twink asked loudly.

"He was playing," his mother said, drying her eyes.

"Look at your face," Twink said. "You can't go out like that!"

Automatically Tommy's mother glanced in the mirror on the living room wall, but she said, "I don't think I want to go, Twink. I don't feel much like a party."

"Now, wait a minute," Twink said angrily. "I went to a lot of trouble to get you invited. This is an important guy. He doesn't have just anyone to his party. You gotta be someone. In this town it's not what you know that gets you work, it's who you know. There'll be a lot of guys there'll help your career."

Tommy had stopped in the doorway to the bedroom. This was the first he'd heard that his mom was going to a party. He was glad she was. She needed to get out, make some more friends. She was lonely without Pete.

"You should go, Mom," he said. "I'll be all right here."

"*Now* you say that," Twink said accusingly. "Look at your mother, crying her eyes out because she thought something had happened to you. If you hadn't been so thoughtless, she'd be all ready to go."

"Don't say that, Twink," his mom said quietly. "It wasn't Tommy's fault. He lost track of the time."

Twink took Tommy's mom's face in her hand, turned it sideways, and said, "Some tea bags on your eyes, ice pack, you'll look fine. Come on now, let's get started. It's nearly eight o'clock. I told Herman I'd be there by eight-thirty. He expects me. Maybe I can be a little late, but he's relying, so we gotta work fast."

"I don't think I want to go," Susan Bridges said. "I think it would be better if I stayed home with Tommy."

Twink Mondragon pursed her lips disagreeably. She folded her hands across her large stomach. "I thought you wanted a career," she said.

"I do," his mom said. "But tonight I don't want to go to a party."

"Listen," Twink said, thrusting one pudgy finger in Susan's direction. "Let me tell you something. In this town, if a girl wants a career, she gets out and gets seen. That's the type of town this is. Don't let that talent stuff fool you. Sure, it helps to have talent, but talent's not what gets you the jobs. It's who you know that gets you the jobs. Taken me twenty . . . er, ten . . . years to find that out. Listen, I want to help you, kid. I want to give you the benefit of my experience. If someone had helped me like I'm helping you, kid, I'd be a star today!"

Having delivered her speech, Twink Mondragon drew back, with her eyes bulging and her lips pressed tight together. Tommy could see that his mom didn't know what to do. She thought she should stay home with him, but she also wanted to go to the party.

"Why don't you go, Mom?" he said. "Have a good time. You need to go to a party. You haven't been out since we . . ."

He stopped just in time. This wasn't the moment to remind her of Pete. But Twink helped. She pounced on his words. "There you are! Even your kid wants you to go out and have a few laughs. Listen," she said to Tommy, "you're not such a bad kid. You tell your mom."

"Go on, Mom," Tommy said. "I can fix my own dinner."

His mom smiled shyly. "You think it would be all right?"

"All right?" demanded Twink, unbuttoning her coat. "Listen, you're entitled!" She threw her coat on a chair. Underneath the coat she was wearing a little black dress with a white collar. "Come on. We've got major work to do if we're going to get you up so they take notice."

She saw Tommy and his mom looking at her dress. She didn't look as though she was dressed to go to a party. She looked like a waitress. "Oh, this," she said, smoothing her dress in embarrassment. "Well, Herman, you know, he's a bachelor and he can't handle it all himself. I sorta help him out."

Tommy's mom burst out laughing. "Twink," she said. "You want me to go to the party as a waitress! Right?"

"No!" Twink Mondragon said, but she avoided looking at either Tommy or Susan. "No, I just sorta help out, that's all."

His mom looked at Tommy and she had the look she had when something was private but funny—the look she gave him sometimes in the supermarket when they got behind someone who made a big fuss. It was a look that said, "This is nuts, but what the hell."

Twink Mondragon was blushing. She looked like she was going to get mad pretty soon, too, particularly if she saw Tommy and his mom laughing at her.

"I try to do something nice for you," she said, "and what thanks do I get?"

"Hey, hey," Susan said. "Don't work yourself up. I'll go."

Twink spun around. "You will?"

"Sure," said Susan. "Why not? I should get out and meet some new people."

"There'll be lots of important people there. It'll help your career, kid, to be seen."

Susan threw Tommy that look again, carefully so that Twink wouldn't see. "Come on," she said to Twink. "You got to help me get ready."

They went into the bedroom and spent some time rummaging in the closet. Tommy got himself a sandwich and a glass of milk. He heard them talking about make-up and jewelry and stuff. He was just finishing his sandwich when they came out of the bedroom. His mom had on a blue dress with long sleeves, no jewelry, and she had her hair hanging down. She looked real young.

Twink rushed over to pick up her coat. "Look at the time! We've got to get our tails out of here."

Susan came over to Tommy. "I love you," she said. "I'm sorry if I got mad. You scared me."

"O.K." Tommy said.

"You lock the door after I'm gone. You don't let anyone in, you hear?"

"Sure, Mom." He could see she was hesitating again, wondering if she should go. "Go on, Mom. Have a good time."

She kissed him on the cheek and followed Twink out of the apartment. He locked the door after her. He heard their footsteps tapping away down the corridor. After they were gone he watched TV for a while, but there were just reruns, so he got bored. He was tired too. He put on his pajamas and went to bed. He lay for a long while thinking about the Indian and Joel way up on the rim of the canyon. He wondered what they were doing and whether they had built a new teepee, and after a while he fell asleep.

The sound of voices woke him up.

His mom was saying, "No, my boy's asleep in the next room."

Then a man said, "You're a class act. I like that."

Then there was some talk he couldn't hear properly but it made him mad anyway. Then the man left. Tommy lay listening to his mom get ready for bed in the next room. He heard her pull down the sofa bed. When she came through the bedroom to go into the bathroom, she came over to the bed and brushed his hair gently with her hand, but he pretended to be asleep. After she had gone back to her own bed, he lay awake for a long time thinking about his mom and the voice in the other room and Pete.

11

FOR TEN DAYS straight Tommy's mom went out every night with Mort Lever. Mort came to the apartment when she got off work at the answering service. He wore jackets with big checks or leisure suits of baby blue, and once he wore something that he called a "jump suit" but looked to Tommy like the type of overalls babies in cribs wore. He was bald on the top of his head, but he grew the hair in back long and combed it to the front to hide his bald spot.

"What do you think of Mort?" his mom asked when she was getting ready to go out on a date.

"He going to get you a job acting?"

His mom pinned her hair up in back. "Oh, I don't know about that," she said. "But he's nice, don't you think?"

Tommy thought he was a creep, but he knew his mom

didn't want to hear that. He said, "He's all right, I guess."

His mom looked at him in the bedroom mirror to see if he was telling the truth, but Tommy looked away quickly. "You all right?"

"Sure, I'm all right," he said.

"You don't mind me going out every night?"

Tommy shrugged, trying to look casual. "Why should I mind?"

"Why don't you have your friend Joel over?" she asked.

Tommy, his mom, Joel, and Little Horse had bumped shopping carts on Thursday in the supermarket at the bottom of the hill. Tommy could tell right off that his mom liked Joel—but then it was hard not to like Joel when he pulled that smile of his. Dressed in his unemployment suit, Little Horse looked nice and square. In a town full of actors with strange names, even "Little Horse" hadn't raised any suspicions in Susan Bridges' mind. Tommy didn't tell her that Joel and Little Horse lived in the estate. He just told her they lived nearby, which wasn't a lie, although it wasn't the whole truth either.

"I don't see much of Joel anymore."

She got up in front of the mirror and picked her evening handbag off the bed. She started filling it with the junk from the bag she used in the day. "Why not? You have a fight?"

Tommy didn't want to answer her. "You going to be late again?" he asked.

His mom laughed. "Hey, guy," she said. "I'm meant to ask *you* that. I'm the grown-up. I say, 'Listen, kid' "—

she pretended to have a deep voice—" 'you be home early, you hear.' " She reached out and ruffled his hair, but he pulled his head away. "Look," she said. "I won't go if it's bothering you. I can call Mort . . ."

"Go!" he said. "Go on. Go out with the creep!"

He ran out of the bedroom and through the living room and grabbed hold of the front door. As he jerked it open he found Mort standing right there with his finger out to push the bell.

"Well, well, well," Mort said. "What have we here?"

"Get lost," Tommy said, and tried to push past him.

Mort took hold of Tommy's arm and held on.

"Let me go!"

"Not so fast, sport," Mort said, and his eyes had narrowed so he didn't look as though he were joking, although the smile stayed on his face. "What did you say?"

"I said you were a creep. A bald-headed creep!"

"Tommy!" his mom said, coming after him. "He didn't mean that, Mort. He's just upset. Tommy, you apologize right away to Mort."

"I apologize, creep," Tommy said, and he jerked his arm free and ran fast as he could down the hall, down the stairs, across the courtyard, and out of the building. He looked left and right on the sidewalk and belted fast up toward the estate, squeezed through the gate, and hid in the gatehouse. He stood there breathing hard, and soon he heard Mort coming.

"He went in here," Mort said. "He had to. If he'd gone down to the boulevard, we'd have seen him. This is the only place he could have gone."

"I'll have to go in," Tommy heard his mom say.

"Are you crazy? That's the old Duggan estate. It's been deserted for years. You'd never find him in there. Look, it's getting dark already. Let him stew for a while. He'll come out as soon as it gets dark."

"We could wait for him in the apartment . . ." his mom said uncertainly.

"Wait nothing. I've got passes to the Bowl tonight. We're going."

"I can't leave him in the dark," his mom said, shocked.

"Look, babe, I've been patient, haven't I?" Mort said. "I mean, I haven't pushed or anything. We've had what, nine, ten dates . . ."

"Ten tonight."

"There you are. Now, I ain't waited that long since I was a kid in school. But I know, you're different. 'She's class,' I said right off. I know you got a kid and you've had a bad time with some old man up north, what the hell, I can wait. But, you know, I'm human too. I've gone to a lot of trouble to get these tickets. I got them because I thought you wanted to go with me."

"Oh, I do."

"Well, then."

There was a long silence, then Susan Bridges said, reluctantly, "If you think it'll be all right. Maybe we could come home early."

"That's my girl," and Tommy heard the sound of a kiss. He wanted to jump right out and pound the hell out of Mort, but Mort was bigger. "I promise. Right after the.

concert we'll come back and I'll tan that little devil's butt if he so much as looks sideways at me."

"Don't you touch Tommy!"

"Sorry, sorry," Mort's voice said. "I won't touch him, I promise. Don't get so het up about it. It does kids good to have a man around. Lord, I can't remember how many times I had my butt pounded by my dad. Did me good."

"Don't ever hit Tommy," his mom said.

"All right, all right," Mort said irritably. "Now let's go."

The light was fading. Ahead of him the trees threw twisted shadows across the driveway. A last bird called out a lonely cry and was silent. Tommy wondered if he should wait a few minutes and go back to the apartment. But his heart was still pounding hard with anger. He was mad and he knew if he went back to the apartment he would sit around and try to watch television and get even more angry. He needed someone to talk to.

The rim of the canyon was a long way up. He searched the night for some sign, a light, that Joel and Little Horse were up there. He didn't want to walk all the way up there and then find that they were gone. The hillside below the rim was dark, almost black, and above it the sky was a midnight blue with lighter spots where the stars were shining. He thought he saw a light right on the rim near the gazebo, but he couldn't be sure. It wasn't dark enough yet to tell what was a star for sure or some other light, a far-off plane making the approach to L.A. International, a searchlight from the valley shooting a column of light up over the hills from the other side, or even just his eyes playing tricks.

He decided to go on up there anyway.

In the ten days that his mother had been going out with Mort, Joel and Little Horse had been setting up camp on the rim of the canyon. When he needed them most to talk to, they hadn't had the time to talk to him. Joel had fixed up the gazebo, closing in the sides with sheets of buckled plywood that he had found abandoned in the scrub. They planted a vegetable garden with seeds that Little Horse bought when he went down to collect his unemployment check. Already the little green fuzz of the sprouting seeds stretched away in long parallel rows beside the gazebo. They had a shower rigged up from one of the old garden taps, and a clothesline stretched between two trees. They had a regular settlement up there and they were enjoying themselves. Tommy felt left out. Every time he went up there, two and three times a day at first, they had something new going, and then after a while they had little jokes of their own, and pretty soon he didn't like going up there at all.

It was almost like losing Pete again, losing Joel. It hurt, so for the last three days he hadn't been up there at all. But tonight he needed someone to talk to, so he hurried up the cracked road that wound around the canyon rim, as night darkened the Los Angeles skyline and, down below, beyond the estate, the city stretched away in rows of lights that marked the streets.

The carved roofline of the gazebo could be seen ahead as a pattern of lace against the sky. There were no other lights to be seen. Tommy began to feel a little afraid. Where would Joel and Little Horse be this late at night? It wasn't late enough to be asleep, but it was too late for them to be down in the lower part of the estate. He slowed his pace, panting from his run, and approached the gazebo carefully. Coming up over the rim of the canyon, he saw the valley on the other side of the hills, revealed suddenly as acres of lights stretching in every direction and, on the horizon, visible only because the sky was now slightly darker than the earth, the red and green lights of a plane winking on and off as it made the approach to the airport. He felt wonderful suddenly, all his anger forgotten, everything forgotten except this wonderful moment when he was standing on the top of the hill and below him for as far as he could see was an ocean of twinkling lights.

He didn't hear anyone coming up behind him, and when the hand was placed across his mouth, his heart stopped for a second and all the strength went out of his arms and legs, and before he got his strength back he felt himself wrestled to the ground with his arms pinned behind his back and a rag pushed into his mouth.

"That's one of the dumber things you've done, kid," Joel said, brushing Tommy off.

"What did you jump on me for?" Tommy asked angrily.

"Thought you were one of those weirdos from the boulevard."

Little Horse came out of the gazebo with a mug in his

hand. "Here," he said. "Drink this. It's orange juice. Make you feel better."

Tommy did as he was told. Nobody had lit any candles, not a lantern, nothing. The ride was in total darkness. Below, the valley lights twinkled on one side. On the other, the deeper darkness of the canyon loomed menacingly, with the road winding down the side like a pale gray snake.

"What would the weirdos be doing up here?" Tommy asked, and he realized that he had been whispering because both Joel and Little Horse were whispering. "I thought they just went up to the old pool."

"They've been coming closer," Joel said, scanning the twisting road. They stood in the shelter of the gazebo, out of the moonlight.

Tommy shivered. "How come?"

"They smell something," Joel said.

"They *smell* something?" Tommy exclaimed in his regular voice.

"Shut *up!*" Joel said, and Tommy could tell from the tone of his voice that he wasn't just trying to be mean. Joel was scared. "Yeah, they smell something, like a coyote smells something on the wind. That type, the weirdos, they've lived so long down there on the streets being treated like animals, eventually they get to thinking like animals, behaving like animals. They know something's going on up here. They sense it."

Little Horse had gone back in the gazebo. "But what?" Tommy asked, looking around at the tiny vegetable garden, the clearing with a couple of benches made of fallen trees, the clothesline. Joel and Little Horse weren't complaining, but they didn't have anything anyone would want to steal. They didn't have money or things that could be sold. They were poor.

Following Tommy's thought, Joel said, "Don't matter that there's nothin' up here they can use. If people kick your butt all the time, pretty soon you're looking for someone else to kick. That's what they want, they want someone else to kick for a while."

Little Horse came back. He spoke quietly. "Maybe we should go up . . . you know."

"Yeah," said Joel, looking about. "Come on," he said to Tommy. "We've got a lookout rigged up."

Tommy followed Joel and Little Horse past the gazebo to the very edge of the canyon wall. There, behind a thick patch of bushes, Joel had set up a lookout post from which you could see all the way back down the road. The three of them crawled in behind the bushes. "Now we wait," Joel said.

For a few minutes, Tommy felt excited. Then as time went by he got bored, and finally he asked, "How long are we going to stay here?"

"All night, if we have to," Little Horse said. "Last night we were here all night."

"Oh," Tommy said, and then, "I can't stay all night. I'll have to go home soon."

"How come you came up here at night, anyway?" Joel whispered. "Won't your mom be looking for you?"

Tommy felt himself flush. "She's gone out," he said.

The way he said it must have told Joel and Little Horse something because Joel asked, "Same guy?"

"Yeah," Tommy said with disgust.

"She must really like him," Joel said. "She's been going out with him a lot, huh?"

"He's a creep!" Tommy said loudly, and both Joel and Little Horse shushed him.

"He's a creep," Tommy repeated quietly.

Nobody said anything for a bit, then Joel said, "Not like Pete?" but he didn't say it as if he wanted to get Tommy mad. He just asked it like a question.

"Naw," Tommy said. "He's real creepy."

"Listen, kid," Little Horse said in a kindly way, "I know how you feel about Pete, but you know, this time it's really not up to you, is it? It's up to your mom. I mean, if she liked Pete, she'd still be up there with him, wouldn't she?"

Tommy didn't want to answer, but he'd come up here to talk to someone, so he eventually said, "She really likes Pete. It's Pete that doesn't like us."

He saw Joel and Little Horse look at each other over his head, so he felt he had to say more. "When they had the fight," he explained with difficulty, because he'd never told anyone this, "Pete told my mom to get out."

Little Horse put his arm around Tommy's shoulder. "That's tough," he said. "Maybe Pete's not such a hot guy, you know. You ever think of that?"

"You don't understand," Tommy said angrily. "Pete

didn't throw us out because he's mean. He told my mom she had to take me and go because . . . because . . ." He couldn't say it.

"Forget it, kid," Little Horse said. "Forget it."

Thinking about it made Tommy think he might cry. He swallowed hard and then he said very quietly, "He told us we had to go because my mom wanted Pete to marry her."

The only sound for a long time after he said that was the wind in the trees down the canyon. Tommy stared hard through the bush of yellow flowers at the long double row of palm trees that lined the driveway far below, and then the thin gray ribbon of road up the canyon. Nothing moved on it.

"Well," Little Horse said after a while in a voice that was tired, real tired, "marriage, you know, it's not for everyone. Others, well, they feel . . . tied down . . . uncomfortable . . . they just can't hack it . . . you can't blame them . . . it's just not for them, marriage. Maybe Pete's one of those guys."

"But why?" Tommy asked out loud, and no one shushed him this time. "What difference would it make? We were all living up there just like they were married anyway. Why wouldn't Pete marry her?"

"Well . . ." Little Horse said, but he couldn't answer.

"He just didn't like us. That's what it was," Tommy said. "That's what I figure." And he'd never told anyone that either. It had taken a long time before he could admit it even to himself.

"No, I don't think that's right," Little Horse said. "I

don't think you've got that right at all, not from what I hear about your mom and Pete. I think this is maybe something else that you don't understand, something personal about Pete."

Joel struck back lightly with his arm right then. "Quiet! Look," he said, and pointed through the bushes way down toward the gate. "They're down there again."

The palm trees swayed in the wind, throwing shadows like huge spears across the estate, making it hard to tell what were bushes and broken walls and low trees and what could be people.

"I don't see anything," Little Horse said.

"Some Indian," Joel scoffed quietly. "Look down there, where the path goes up to the pool house."

Tommy and Little Horse leaned forward, craning their necks in the direction Joel pointed. Out from the shadows came five figures, half dancing, half walking. They darted from one side of the path to the other. Not a sound came up from below.

"They're going the other way," Little Horse said. "They're going up to the old pool."

"Tonight," Joel said. "One of these times soon they're going to come looking for us."

"I'll beat the hell out of the little punks," Little Horse said.

Joel said nothing. He watched the shadowed figures disappear around the path in the other direction. "Lot of them," he said. "Five, maybe more."

"Kids," Little Horse said.

"Some kids are more dangerous than others," Joel said.

"Some grow up real mean. Me, I think maybe we better be ready to run like hell if they come up this way."

They sat there squashed together for some time before Joel said, "All right. They ain't comin' up tonight." Tommy's legs felt as though they'd gone to sleep. Little Horse had to help him out of the bush. Clouds were coming in from the ocean now. They passed in front of the moon, scudding along before the wind, plunging the landscape into sudden darkness, then lighting it fast again like a flash bulb.

"Storm," Little Horse said.

Joel looked at him in surprise. "Right on, Old Indian Weatherman. You're beginning to talk like a country boy."

"That's the problem with you country brats," Little Horse said. "You think you know it all. You don't have to be a country boy to know a storm's coming up. Any damn fool city boy could tell you that."

"Be good for the brush," Joel said. "Tinder's dry right now. Take a good two-day rain to make it safe again."

"Listen," Little Horse said to Tommy. "I think I better get you home. Getting late."

"They've gone to the Bowl," Tommy said. "They won't be home for a long time."

"Just the same," Little Horse said. "I'll take you down. I don't want to get caught down there in the rain or"—he looked at Joel—"in any other way," and Tommy knew he meant the weirdos from the boulevard. "Let's go."

"I'll stay up here," Joel said. "Tie a few things down." He looked up at the sky again. "Coming down from the north," he said. "Won't get here right away, maybe even a day or two, depending on the wind. Just the same, a good wind could blow this whole place away." He looked around at the gazebo and the vegetable garden, the clothesline and all the rest, with pride, as though it was the first home he'd ever had, the first home he really cared about.

"Sure enough," Little Horse said. "I'll take Tommy down. Be back soon."

They started off down the ribbon road. Above them the moon appeared and disappeared as the clouds floated by overhead, showing them the road one minute, leaving them in shadow the next. Going down was a lot faster than going up.

"Listen," Little Horse said, speaking quietly as they got closer to the canyon floor. "You don't do anything dumb to your mom, you hear?"

"It's not me who's doing something dumb," Tommy said. "It's her that's maybe going to do something dumb."

"Go easy on her," Little Horse said. "She's lonely, too, you know. Kids aren't the only people who get lonely."

Tommy knew he was right, but he didn't say anything. Lots of thoughts were in his mind. Some of them felt sorry for his mom and some of them were as mad as a hornet at her. Some of them were even mad at Pete, and he'd never been mad at Pete ever.

They had come to the fork in the road. He knew Little Horse was going to say some more things to him, but he didn't want to hear them. "I can go the rest of the way from here," he said.

"I better take you all the way," Little Horse said.

"I can do it!" Tommy said, and Little Horse stopped.

"O.K." He took a step back. "Look, if you need someone to talk to, come up and see us. Not tomorrow. Tomorrow's unemployment day. I put on the old suit and go on down to see the Man tomorrow, then we go to the stores. Takes just about all day, but day after we'll be right up there on top of the world." He waved at the gazebo. Tommy could tell it was making Little Horse as happy as Joel, and suddenly he felt a pain, real sharp, of jealousy that everyone had someone—his mom and Mort, Little Horse and Joel—and he was left out. He didn't wait to thank Little Horse for bringing him down, but turned quickly and ran off down the rest of the path to where the trees formed a dark tunnel that led to the gate.

"I tell you, man," a voice said from the end of the tunnel. "I seen 'em."

Tommy stepped off the path into the trees and pressed back as far as he could. He was afraid to step too far back off the path because the ground under the trees was covered with dry leaves that would rustle and give him away to the figures coming fast up through the tunnel.

"I saw 'em," the voice rasped. "This real strange dude dressed up like some TV Indian and a kid."

"You think they're hidin' out here?" a second voice asked excitedly.

"Who knows, man, what they're up to. But if they live up here, I'm goin' to find them. And there ain't but one way out of this canyon."

The two speakers passed right by Tommy, brushing within inches of him. It was dark in the tunnel of trees, but he could see that they were young, about Joel's age, but dirty and untidy. He could smell them as they went by. They laughed suddenly and Tommy shivered right down into his sneakers because the laughs were high and thin and echoed in the tunnel like the screech of bats. Then they were past him and moving out into the estate.

He stood for a few seconds waiting to see if there were any more coming. His heart slowed to its regular pace, and he thought maybe he should go back in the estate and warn Little Horse and Joel. But he didn't know where the two boys had gone. They might be hiding out along the path and then they'd catch him before he got a chance to warn the two guys up at the gazebo. They were way up there where they could see everything. He figured they'd be O.K., and it wouldn't do them any good if he went in and got captured, so he waited a few minutes more to make sure the coast was clear and then ran as if a pack of dogs were at his heels, down the last few yards of the path, through the gate and back down the street to the apartment building.

Much later he heard his mom come into his room. She tucked the covers around his neck.

"He's asleep," she whispered.

"I knew he'd come back. You see, we didn't have to leave the Bowl early."

"You're good to me, Mort. I was worried."

"When you going to start being good to me, eh?"

He heard his mom kiss Mort then. "Soon," she said. "I appreciate you being so patient."

"You want to take in a show tomorrow night, maybe go back to my place later?"

His mom hesitated. "Tommy . . ." she said.

"We'll get Twink to come over and babysit. What do you say?"

After a couple of seconds his mom said, "All right," but slowly, as though she wasn't really happy about the idea.

"I'll talk to Twink," Mort said briskly. "I'll set it all up."

Then Tommy heard him kiss her again, and the front door closed. His mom took her time changing into her nightdress. He heard the couch being folded down into a bed and then his mom came through the bedroom to clean her teeth. She checked on Tommy on her way through, touching his forehead lightly with her fingers. She went back to her own bed, leaving the door open between the rooms, and shut off the light. Tommy lay awake for a long time. Sometime around dawn he made his decision: he'd run away.

12

THE STORM HESITATED out over the ocean waiting to come in. Tommy stood under the palm trees in Santa Monica Park staring out at the clouds piling up over the ocean and the bank of fog that clung around the pier. The waves were gray with whitecaps. To his right was the road that ran down to the highway and behind him San Vicente Boulevard. He'd used his last money to get this far. If he was going any further he had to go down there on the highway and stick his thumb out.

The wind cut through his windbreaker. He shivered. It was six-thirty in the morning. The only other person in the park was a drunk wrapped in newspapers huddled by the men's room, which was locked.

"Once you make up your mind," Pete's voice said in his memory, "don't worry about it anymore. Just follow through with your decision. But think about it real hard before you make that important decision."

"Well, he'd thought about it. He'd thought about it all night and he'd decided. Before he left he'd taken his mom's lipstick and written in big letters across the wall: "Mort is a Creep." That was dumb. That was kid stuff and he was sorry now that he'd done it. But it was done and he couldn't worry about that anymore. He had other problems now, like how to get on up the highway before the storm rolled in. He was only cold now; once the storm hit, he'd be wet, too. He wanted to be on his way to Santa Barbara before the rain came.

He was on his way to see Pete.

The highway was polished slick with the morning mist. The beach club buildings across the road loomed up out of the fog like a huge white ship, all wood, with turrets and terraces running along above the beach. The tennis courts were walled with green canvas and wire. Sea gulls sat along the wire with their necks pulled down into their feathers, looking gloomily out at where the ocean should be. It was very quiet; the only sounds were the sea rolling into the beach and the swish of car tires on the wet pavement.

There wasn't much traffic. Most of it was coming into town, people coming in from Malibu to work at the studios. The traffic going out of town was mostly trucks, not many of them, rolling up the highway with a whine of changing gears. They made a huge racket for a couple of seconds and then they were gone, taking their noise with them.

Tommy stood by the side of the road where he could be seen but wasn't in any danger of being hit by one of the trucks. He held his arm out and his thumb cocked in the direction of Santa Barbara, north. The wind whipped at his jacket and he hunched his shoulders like the gulls. The trucks went by, the drivers high up in their cabs, riding above everyone else. Nobody stopped.

His teeth started to chatter. He looked out at the clouds. The sun was out there trying to fight its way through, but you wouldn't have known it. The clouds were piled up gray and black. Thunder boomed out in the cloud bank, and then the clouds paled as the lightning struck down through them. Tommy turned and started to walk up the highway. At least when he walked he wasn't cold. When he heard a car or a truck coming, he'd turn and stick out his thumb, but they went right on by. He walked up past beach restaurants, Will Rogers Beach with the empty parking lot, past the vollyball net hanging wet from the fog, and along onto the empty highway. No rides. His jacket soaked up the moisture in the air. He shoved his hands deeper into the pockets of the windbreaker. The cold wasn't going to stop him, he told himself. Even the storm wouldn't stop him. He was going to talk to Pete. There were lots of things he didn't understand, things he had to have an answer to. Like why did his mom need someone like Mort? Tommy knew she was lonely. He was lonely too, Tommy was, and he needed friends, but . . . but what? That was what he had to know. Tommy had to talk to Pete.

He heard the truck coming up behind him and turned

wearily to stick out his thumb. He didn't expect anything anymore. He'd been out on the highway nearly an hour. He'd walked half the fifteen miles to Malibu. At the rate he wasn't getting rides, he'd have to walk the whole ninety miles to Santa Barbara. Ninety miles was a long way without any money, and without money he couldn't eat and . . . "When there's no choice," Pete used to say, "you just go ahead and don't think about it . . ."

To his surprise the truck started to slow down. It was a big yellow Mack pulling an eight-wheel trailer. The driver geared down, slowing the great beast to a crawl. Tommy stepped further off the highway as the truck pulled over, rolling past him before it stopped. He ran after the truck fast and as he came up to the cab the door was thrown open.

"Hop in," the driver said.

Tommy climbed up into the cab. He slammed the door. The driver was a middle-aged man with a large pot belly that stuck out over his pants. He took a cigar butt out of the ashtray and stuck it in the corner of his mouth. He threw the truck into gear and they pulled out slowly onto the highway.

The first raindrops splashed on the windshield, great fat wet ones. "Hell of a storm comin'," the driver said. "Where you goin'?"

"Santa Barbara."

"You're in luck," the driver said. "I'm goin' right through."

The radio crackled. He put his cigar back into the ashtray and picked up the receiver. "Big Bopper, Big Bopper," he said. "Comin' out of Shaky City on the Coast Highway. What's ahead?"

He switched to receive. The windshield wipers went back and forth twice and then the radio crackled again. "Kayo Kid," the radio said. "Kayo Kid, up Number One comin' down from Bay City. Like a skatin' rink up here. Stay out of the fifty-dollar lane. The smokies are sittin' waitin' to be fed. Over."

A car ahead of the truck skidded sideways on the slick highway. The driver applied the brakes carefully. The driver up in front got control and pulled away.

"Big Bopper," the radio said. "Comin' in for Java?"

"Got a truckin' teen," the driver told him. "We'll just boogie on through. Eighty-eights. Kayo."

"Eights and other good numbers, good buddy. Pack it up."

The driver hung the radio transmitter back on its hook. "So," he said, picking up his dead cigar again. "You goin' home?"

"Sort of," Tommy said evasively. "What's Shaky City?"

"C.B. talk for L.A."

"And the smokies are the cops?"

"Right you are," the guy said with a grin. "And the fifty-dollar lane?"

"The fast lane."

"You're a smart kid. Goin' home?" he repeated.

"Going to visit a friend," Tommy said.

The driver looked at him and then back at the road. The rain washed across the highway in curtains of water.

"Okay," he said. "Have it your way. Just take care, that's all. The road's no place for a kid your age."

"I'm thirteen," Tommy said.

"I'm nearer fifty," the driver said, "and I'm not sure it's any place for me, either."

Then the road took his attention. The wipers worked double time and the rain poured down the windshield in torrents. The day went from light to dark, and the driver turned on the headlights. Cars came at them, lights burning like two yellow eyes, creeping along in the storm. Visibility was less than a hundred feet. They passed up through Malibu, Pirate's Cove, and across to Number One. They'd been on the road an hour before they got as far as Oxnard, another half hour to Ventura. The storm blew all around, thrashing the fields, beating the lettuce crop flat, shaking the tomatoes off the vines, whipping the artichoke bushes ragged. The wires of the telephone poles vibrated in the wind. The birds took shelter. Nothing could be seen of the Pacific except the banks of dark clouds coming in, roll on roll like the waves themselves.

"I got two kids," the driver said after a long silence.

"Oh, yeah?" Tommy said.

"Twelve and fourteen."

Tommy didn't say anything. He listened. He knew he was going to be told something more.

"Twelve and fourteen," the driver repeated. "Good kids."

The wind hit a Volkswagen in the oncoming lane. The little car spun across the highway and onto the shoulder.

"Damn fool," the driver said. "Those pregnant roller skates should be banned from the road."

They drove along for a couple more miles and then he said, "I always worry, you know, 'bout my kids. All this takin' off, hittin' the road. I see lots of kids, try to give them a ride, ask them if they're all right. Never know, one day might be one of my own. In my day," he said kind of sadly, "kids stayed home till they got out of school. Nowadays, you're lucky if you bat one out of two. Right now we're battin' real lucky with ours. You know what I'm sayin', kid?"

Tommy blushed. "I'm not running away," he lied, and even as he said it he could feel his face getting hot. "I'm goin' to see my dad." He said it loudly, defiantly, but as he said it his voice cracked and it sounded like the lie it was.

The driver looked at him for a second and then back at the road. "Whatever you say." The highway wound out to the shore again. Way ahead the lights of the oil rigs burned dimly out in the channel. The waves were pounding on the breakwater. Lightning struck, turning the scene white.

"Santa Barbara round the next bend," the driver said.

"Yeah, I know," Tommy said. "You can let me off anywhere this side of town."

The truck pulled up over the last rise and there down below were the outskirts of town, the long row of shacks and, beyond them, the big houses of the rich, and far away the lights of the Coral Casino Club and the Biltmore

Hotel. Their lights glistened in the rain, and smoke came out of the chimneys on the roofs of some of the shacks. Tommy felt his heart swell with a sudden happiness like Christmas, or coming home, or something wonderful, because somewhere up there was Pete, and if he wasn't in the shack, he soon would be, because the storm would bring him in early. Just looking at the town in the rain made him feel good, better than he'd felt in a long time.

"Anywhere here," he said.

The driver slowed the truck. He pulled the long rig off the road. With the engine idling, they could hear the whine of the wind, the anger of the storm outside, the machine-gun play of the raindrops on the roof.

"Thanks," Tommy said.

"You're sure you're expected?" the driver asked.

"I'm just going over the highway," Tommy insisted. "That's where my dad lives," and to show he meant what he said he opened the door on his side. The wind came in with a chill blast and, with it, the rain. Tommy jumped down. He turned to say thanks again.

The driver leaned over the seat. "Here you are, kid," he said, holding out a dollar. "You might need some change to call home."

"I don't need it," Tommy shouted up into the rain. "My dad's here."

"Take it!" the driver said, waving the bill at him.

Tommy reached up and took the dollar. "Thanks," he said.

"These are tough times for kids," the driver said, reaching over to take hold of the door handle. "I always think it might be one of my own one day. Take care, son."

He slammed the door. Tommy stepped back. The monster truck lumbered slowly forward gaining speed, pulled out, and was on its way, the taillights glowing in the rain.

Tommy watched the truck until it was lost in the storm, then he checked the highway left and right and ran across. On the other side, he strained to see if there was a light in the shack, but the wind stung his eyes and the rain ran down his face as though he were crying. The shack sat down by the edge of the water, sandwiched between two others. Wiping his eyes, he looked again and made out the patch on the roof where he and Pete had fixed the shakes when the big storm last summer tore some loose, and then he saw there was a light in the window, so he knew Pete was home. He slid down the sand dunes, tore off his sneakers, and ran barefoot toward the shack, toward Pete, and as he ran he started to laugh with happiness, his hair flat on his head from the rain and the water running down his face.

"Pete," he called. "Pete. I'm back!"

13

THE DOOR OPENED. A figure with the light behind it filled the frame.

Tommy took a step back. "Pete?"

Pete came out into the storm. "Tommy?"

Tommy ran forward. "Pete," he said. "I ran away. I came back."

The waves crashed in on the beach behind them, lapping up the sand, sucked back into the ocean, and then crashed against the beach again, reaching further.

Pete pulled Tommy into the shack. He shut the door with difficulty and suddenly everything seemed quiet. The storm hammered on the door, and the fire in the small grate flickered from the wind pushing back down the stovepipe chimney.

"You better change," Pete said. "You'll catch your

death of cold dressed like that. I think maybe there's still some of your clothes around here . . ." He looked vaguely around the untidy room as though he might see them. He pushed aside a pile of his own clothes, stared hard at a stack of books, and then said, "There are some here somewhere. I saw them the other day. I was going to send them to you."

Tommy shivered. "I'll get a towel," he said, and went through to the little bedroom. Pete's bedroom was as untidy as the living room. For some reason that made Tommy feel good. He went into the tiny bathroom. The towels had always been stacked on a shelf there. Today there was just a pile of used towels in a corner, and one that was still wet draped across the shower curtain. Tommy took that down, took off his clothes, and started to dry himself.

Pete pushed open the curtain. "Here," he said. "Dry yourself on this." He handed Tommy a clean sheet. "I haven't got to the laundry lately," Pete said. Pete looked tired. Tommy had always remembered Pete as smiling, as happy, but today he looked tired. And Tommy couldn't ever remember the shack being this untidy. Pete had always said, "When you live in a small place—and we live in a very small place—you got to be twice as tidy as anywhere else." Tommy wondered what the boat looked like. Pete had been a fanatic about keeping the boat neat. "Everything has to go back in its place," he used to say. "In an emergency, you have no time to search for things. You have to be able to reach for them and find them where they're supposed to be."

When he came out of the small bathroom space, Tommy saw some of his old clothes piled on the end of the unmade bed. He'd grown since he'd worn those jeans. He had to squeeze into them, but the sweatshirt fit. He opened a drawer and took out a pair of Pete's socks. They were much too big for him, but they were warm.

Pete was stoking up the fire in the other room. He looked around. "I put some food on for you."

Tommy felt shy suddenly. He wanted to explain. "I had to talk to you."

Pete poked at the wood. "Your mom know you're here?"

"That's what I wanted to talk to you about."

The rain lashed at the windows. Pete said, "She'll be plenty worried. We should go phone her."

"Still no phone?" Tommy asked, teasing. His mom had wanted a telephone. She'd bugged Pete about that for two years, but Pete always refused.

"No," Pete said, with the first smile he'd shown since Tommy arrived. "But I've been thinking about getting one."

"Pete! You always said telephones bring more bad news than good. 'A man's better off without a telephone.' That's what you always said."

"Yeah, I said a lot of things," Pete said. "I've talked a fair amount of baloney, I guess. Hope you didn't listen to too much of it. Ready to eat?"

Tommy nodded. Pete went over to the hot plate. "Stew," he said. "Out of a can. Not like your mom's."

He ladled it out and brought it back to Tommy by the

fire. Steam rose out of the bowl. Pete hadn't asked how his mom was, so Tommy said, "Mom misses you."

Pete's expression changed. He was a big man. He'd spent most of his life out on boats. His face had a weather tan, not just the sun but the wind, so he was brown all year, but he looked pale and unhappy now. Tommy had never seen Pete like this. "She misses you," he repeated.

Pete turned away. "I miss her," he said softly. "But, you know, sometimes people have to go their own way."

Tommy put the bowl of stew on the table. "Why?" he asked. "Why can't you be together? Don't you like us anymore?" That was a kid-stuff thing to ask, and even as he said it he thought so, but that was what he wanted to know. That was what he had come to ask Pete. He rushed on before Pete could tell him to grow up and stop whining. "She's seeing this really dumb guy and I know she doesn't really like him but she's lonely. She wants *you*, Pete."

Pete didn't say anything. He started to pick up clothes off the floor.

"*I* want you, Pete," Tommy said, feeling really like a kid now, a dumb little kid. But when Pete and his mom had had the fight, he'd acted like a grown-up, said nothing, left them alone to work out their own fight, and what had happened? They'd ended split up. He didn't care if he was acting like a kid. He had things he had to say, things he should have said before.

Without turning, Pete said, "You gotta learn that there are lots of things in life that you'll want that you can't have."

"You always said . . ." Tommy started.

Pete turned on him. "Will you stop telling me what I always said?" he shouted.

Tommy felt as though he'd been slapped. He sat right back in the chair. The wind slammed something against the shack. They stared at each other, saying nothing for a long minute.

"Jeez, I'm sorry, Tommy," Pete said. "I'm sorry. Eat your food."

Tommy picked up the spoon and pushed the food around in the bowl. "How's the boat?" he asked eventually.

"Awful," Pete said. "I practice the breaststroke every morning before I go out. One of these days when I'm diving I'm going to look around and find the *Lazy Gal* sittin' right there on the bottom beside the abalone."

Tommy laughed. "Aw, come on," he said. "The *Lazy Gal*'s a terrific boat."

Pete went on picking up things off the floor. Now he had a whole pile of them in his arms. He looked at them as if he didn't know what to do with them, and he dropped them in the corner.

"I'd come back," Tommy said in a low voice.

Pete looked at him. "You got to go to school."

"I'm thirteen," Tommy said. "That's old enough to quit school."

"Like hell it is."

"You quit school when you were fourteen," Tommy reminded him.

"That was a long time ago," Pete said, moving around

the small room like a caged animal. "And look what it got me anyway." He waved at the mess. "This."

"This is great," Tommy said.

"Oh, sure. At thirteen it's great. At thirty-eight . . ." Pete made a face. "At thirty-eight it's maybe not so great."

"It's great!" Tommy insisted. "You always said . . ." Pete looked at him warningly. "You always said," Tommy repeated defiantly, "that it's not what a guy has that's important, it's how he feels about himself."

"I guess what I'm saying, then, is that right now I'm not feeling so good about myself," Pete said. "Will you eat up? Look at that. I go and make you a terrific bowl of canned stew and you just sit there pushing it around."

"You were right," Tommy said. "It's not as good as Mom's."

"Don't pull that one, Tommy," Pete warned him.

Tommy ate his stew. The big man prowled around the shack, going from one room to the other, moving things, cleaning up a bit. Outside, the storm was rising. The rain washed down the windows.

Pete came back into the front room. "So who's this guy Susan's seeing?" he demanded.

"Just some guy."

"Oh," Pete said, and he went back into the bedroom and banged some drawers. Pretty soon he was back. "What guy?"

"Some guy," Tommy said. "He's a creep."

"How a creep?"

"He's an accountant."

Pete laughed. "That makes him a creep?"

"He wants her to . . . you know . . ."

"What?"

"You know . . ."

Pete got an angry look on his face. "It's her life," he said, slamming out of the room. Tommy took his empty bowl over to the sink and put it on top of the others. He ran some water in the sink and started to do the dishes.

"That's the first time you ever did that without having to be asked," Pete said.

Tommy shrugged. "I'm growing up."

He washed some plates, rinsed them, and stacked them in the rack. "Pete, can I ask you something?"

"What? Sure." Pete slumped in the chair by the fire.

"Don't you like us anymore?"

This time it was Pete who looked as if he had been hit. His face changed, looked hurt, and he turned away. "Sure, I like you, Tommy," he said with his back turned. "I like you and Susan a lot."

Tommy soaped a dish for a few minutes. "Well, when did you stop *loving* Mom, then?"

Pete stared into the fire. "You've got it wrong. It wasn't like that. We wanted different things. That was what it was."

"Like what?"

"You wouldn't understand."

Tommy threw the dish into the suds. "You said you'd always tell me the truth! You said you'd never say I wouldn't understand!"

"Your mother wanted me to marry her!" Pete yelled. "That's what the problem was!"

In the silence that followed the wind shrieked around the roof.

"Then you *didn't* love her anymore," Tommy said.

"Of course I love her," Pete said, getting out of the chair in exasperation.

"Then why wouldn't you marry her?"

"Because I'd always told her I wouldn't," Pete explained with his jaw set in the stubborn way he had when he was mad. "I told her that right at the beginning. She knew that. That was our deal. Listen," he said, looking around the room as though he was hoping to find an escape, "I've got to go down to the boat."

"I'll go with you," Tommy said.

"No!" It was an order, almost a shout. "No. You stay here. You've already been soaked. You'd catch a cold."

"Bull," Tommy said, and stepped back quickly because he saw Pete's hand bunch into a fist. "You don't want me with you."

From the back of the door Pete took down a rain slicker. "That's enough," he said.

Tommy suddenly knew something that shocked him. He didn't want to say it but he knew this might be his last chance. "You're afraid," he said.

For a minute Pete just continued pulling the slicker over his turtleneck.

"You're a coward," Tommy said.

"Enough," Pete shouted. "You, you're just a kid. What right do you have to go around telling people what they should do and what they shouldn't?"

Tommy backed away. But he spoke up. "You're afraid

to marry Mom. You're afraid she'll tie you down, then you won't be able to run away if things get tough, if you lose the boat. All that stuff you talked, all that stuff you told me, that was all talk . . . and I believed you."

A log fell out of the fire. Pete looked at it as it rolled onto the floor. He didn't move. "A man can't always be as good as he'd like to be," he said. "You'll learn that."

"Not from you," Tommy said. "I've learned enough from you."

"Pick up the log, will you?" Pete asked him.

"Pick it up yourself," Tommy said.

Pete moved so fast he was across the room before Tommy knew what was about to happen. Pete cuffed him one on the ear. "Listen, you. I didn't ask you up here. You came up here on your own. If I have problems with myself, you invited yourself into them. Now, you pick up that damn log."

The log was burning a hole in the old rug. Neither of them moved. "Oh, hell," Pete said, and bent and picked the log up by the end that wasn't burning and put it back on the fire.

When Pete had done that, Tommy felt ashamed of himself. "I'm sorry, Pete," he said. "You always told me . . ." he hesitated before he finished, but then he went on, ". . . you always told me a man shouldn't get himself boxed in by his own pride."

"Not pride that's the trouble," Pete said. "Look at this place. Sure I need Susan, but what could I offer her? When we all lived here together, it was like a holiday, right? A long holiday. We get married . . . that's responsibilities." He stared hard at Tommy. "Maybe even more children, who knows? I don't know if I'm ready for that."

The waves out on the beach hit the sand with a slap like a gunshot. Both Pete and Tommy jumped. They looked at each other sheepishly.

"If you don't take any chances . . ." Tommy began.

". . . you never get anywhere," Pete finished. "I know. I wrote that line, I remember."

"You know what I think?" Tommy asked.

"I don't think I want to hear it right this minute," Pete said.

"I think it's dumb. You're unhappy, Mom's unhappy, I'm unhappy, and why? Because *you* won't grow up. You want to be a kid forever, go around talking big but never taking on any responsibilities. Everybody's got to be unhappy just so Big Man Pete can be free."

Pete was mad again. "I'm going to go down the road to the tavern, call your mom, tell her you're all right."

"If you don't take a chance," Tommy said desperately, "you're going to end up with nothing. You're going to end up all alone."

The muscles on Pete's jaw were clenched. His shoulders bunched under the rain slicker. "Right now, being alone sounds like a fine state." He pulled the door open. The wind rushed in, knocking magazines off tables, glasses, newspapers, rolling the rug toward the fire. The curtains blew and the rain washed against the sill, and then the door shut and Pete was gone and with him the angry wind.

Tommy listened to the storm for a while. He cleaned

up the shack some. Every now and then he would stop in his chores and say, "Nuts!" He didn't know if he had done right or wrong arguing with Pete. Maybe Pete was right after all. Maybe Tommy *was* just a kid and didn't know enough. When the small shack was a bit tidier, he raked the fire down to a bed of coals. Then he made up the cot he'd always slept on in the living room and lay down on it. He lay there for a long, long time listening to the rain on the roof and the waves on the beach, the wind howling and the odd thump as something hit the side of the shack. He fell asleep.

Pete came home hours later. He crept in, trying not to wake Tommy, went into the bedroom, and closed the door. Tommy listened to him pacing the floor, back and forth for another hour as though he was thinking hard. Then the long day caught up with Tommy and he slipped back down into a hard sleep where he dreamed the sun was shining and there were no problems and everyone got along fine.

14

BUT IN THE morning the rain hammered on the roof harder than ever. Pete came into the front room to stoke the fire. Tommy thought that if only his mom were there, if it were all the way it used to be, this could have been one of those great rainy days when they all stayed home together and his mom made a meat loaf for dinner and Pete worked on his accounts, trying to figure out if he could afford to fix the *Lazy Gal* up some, and Tommy lay around on the floor playing at doing his schoolwork but mostly just feeling good, feeling safe and warm and happy.

"Hey, you," Pete called. "Out of bed."

"It's warm in here," Tommy said. "Think I'll just stay here till you get the fire going." Then he lay back and waited. He didn't have to wait long, maybe ten seconds, before Pete was by the side of the cot. "Out!" he said. "If I'm freezing my tail out here, you're going to freeze your tail."

"Doesn't make any sense both of us freezing our tails," Tommy said, pulling the blankets up to his chin and being careful to keep the smile hidden. "Best you freeze your tail since you're already up. Call me when breakfast is ready."

Pete grabbed hold of the blanket and pulled it down. "Out!"

"No, no, no," Tommy said. He grabbed hold of the blanket, trying to pull it back, but now Pete had him down on the bed, tickling him. "No fair, no fair," Tommy called. "You know I'm ticklish. Oh, Pete, please, no, I'll get up. I will, I will!"

"Right you will," Pete said, laughing. "Or it's into a nice cold rain shower for you."

"Bully!" Tommy said as he got out of bed.

"What?" asked Pete with a smile as he opened the door on the storm. The cold wind tore around the room, shaking the curtains, tossing papers across the floor. Rain stained a pattern on the doorstep.

"Your fire's out," Tommy said.

Pete closed the door. He stoked up the fire again while Tommy dressed in his clothes that had dried overnight. Pete whistled all the while, and then he started on breakfast, banging the iron skillet on the old stove just as he used to do on Sundays in the old days when Mom stayed in bed and Pete and Tommy fixed breakfast.

"You talk to Mom?" Tommy asked.

"Hmmmmm . . ." Pete said.

He put on bacon, asked Tommy how many eggs he wanted, put the toast in the toaster. Tommy tidied up the room.

"What's he like?" Pete asked when they were sitting across from each other at the table. "This guy Susan's been seeing."

"He's just some guy," Tommy said.

"He must be like something," Pete said.

"Not as tall as you," Tommy said.

Pete ate his eggs for a few seconds. "Fun?"

"I guess Mom thinks so."

Pete broke his bacon up into little pieces the way he did when he was worried. "How old is he?"

"Old," Tommy said. "Forty maybe."

"I'm thirty-eight," Pete said, mashing the bacon into crumbs.

Tommy didn't reply. He watched Pete closely. They finished their breakfast in silence. Pete's good mood was gone. The rain washed down the windows, soaked under the door, began to drip through the roof in one corner. Pete looked at all the water morosely, and said, "This is no place for a man to live."

"It's the best place I ever lived!" Tommy said fiercely.

That seemed to soften Pete up a bit. He rubbed Tommy's head once and said, "We had some good times, didn't we?" but he didn't want an answer, for he turned away quickly and went back into the bedroom to change his clothes.

He still had the old truck. They climbed into that and

sat out there under the shelter while the engine warmed up a bit. "Before I take you back to the city, I should go down to the *Gal*," Pete said. "You mind?"

"I'd really like to see the *Gal*," Tommy said, feeling the heat in the truck warm his feet. "You think she'll make another season?"

For as long as he'd known Pete that had been the big question, whether his boat, which he had bought with the money he'd saved up in the Navy and had nursed along ever since, would survive another fishing season. There never seemed to be enough money to put a down payment on a new boat, so he patched the old one year after year and said, "Maybe next year I can get another boat."

"She's got to make it," Pete said. "I've got some money saved, a little. If I can just get by one more season I think maybe I could put something down on a new boat."

He backed the truck out of the shelter. The road was slick with rain. They bumped along the highway toward the fishing marina.

"Pete," Tommy asked. He didn't know how to go on.
"What?"

Tommy looked out the window as he spoke. "You think maybe I could come work on the *Gal* next summer when school's out?"

He kept looking the other way till Pete spoke. After a wait, Pete said, "Well, I don't know, Tommy, you're awful young . . ."

"I'm thirteen!" Tommy protested. "Next summer I'll be fourteen. I can do the work of a man. Well, almost. Anyway, you wouldn't have to pay me much, so you'd save more money for a new boat, and I know the *Gal*, you know that."

"I'll think about it."

"That means no."

Pete turned the truck onto the old wooden dock, driving carefully down the center out of long habit to avoid the ridges where the tracks had run in the old days when trains pulled out along the dock to load the boats. That had stopped long ago and now there were just the ruts in the planking where the rails had been.

"Don't know what's gonna give up first," Pete said. "The dock or the *Gal*."

Tommy saw the mast of the *Gal* rocking back and forth in the wind, and then the *Lazy Gal* herself bobbing high at anchor out in the channel. The waves buffeted her as they pushed in to shore, and she swung around on her anchor chain, taking the worst of the storm with her stern. "She looks beautiful," Tommy said. "The *Gal* will always be my favorite boat."

"Yeah," Pete said fondly. "She's one hell of a little scow. She's treated us well."

Pete pulled the truck to one side of the dock and they got out. They climbed down the ladder into the dinghy with the rain running down their faces, their parkas soaked, and rowed out to the little boat. Tommy held the dinghy steady alongside while Pete climbed on board. He checked the anchor chains, went below to make sure everything was stowed safely, and came back to the dinghy. They rowed back to the dock, tied up, and climbed back up into the truck.

They dried their faces on a towel they'd brought along, and shucked off the wet parkas. Pete had left the engine running. The truck was warm inside.

"Next stop L.A.," Pete said, turning the truck around on the dock.

"Shaky City."

"Huh?"

"Shaky City. That's what C.B.'ers call Los Angeles."

Pete laughed. "Kinda fits, doesn't it?"

The storm clouds hung low over the town. They drove through the deserted lower town, past the railway station, and out onto the freeway. The wind, driving the rain ahead of it, shook the truck like a buggy. Pete held tight to the wheel, driving carefully on the slick road.

"Looks clear ahead," he said.

Down the highway in the direction of the city, the sky was blue and clear. "This storm'll blow down that way by tonight," Pete said. "It'll move right along behind us."

The warmth of the truck and Pete beside him made Tommy feel happy. He didn't want to think about what was ahead. He didn't want to think about L.A. or his mom or any of that. He just wanted the ride to go on for a long time, but just as Pete said, they drove out of the storm around Malibu and the traffic became heavier, more frantic, cars going by fast on both sides. Pete got nervous because he wasn't used to the traffic, and pretty soon the warm, good feeling was gone.

"This is no place to live," Pete said.

Tommy didn't answer him. What could he say? He could say, "You're right, Pete, but then you've got a choice. You can live up the coast and fish and live in the shack. A kid, he has to go where he's told." What was the good of saying that? That would just make Pete more up-tight, so Tommy said nothing, the way he'd learned to say nothing to his mom when she got mad, not at him, but at herself, or other people, the telephone company, the land-lord. When adults talked like that, they were just talking. They didn't really want a conversation.

They turned off up Coldwater and into Beverly Hills. The big houses of the rich people were on either side of the road, huge houses with neat, smooth lawns, and Tommy thought about Joel, who wanted so badly to live in one of those houses that he'd lied about it and pre-tended that he did.

Pete started to laugh. "Man," he said, "some people are even bigger fools than you and me, Tommy," he said. "Look at these houses. Can you imagine what a guy could get with the money they spend on these houses? You could get a terrific boat, the best boat in the world with the money one of these things cost. With a boat like that a guy could sail all around the world."

They crossed the Beverly Hills city limit. Then they were in Hollywood getting close to the apartment, and Tommy felt his stomach tighten and he had to concentrate hard at not getting uptight himself.

"Look," Pete said. "What did I tell you? There's the storm clouds moving in," and he pointed up toward the hills behind the apartments.

Those clouds are coming the wrong way, Tommy thought. *They're coming from the hills. They should be*

(*121*)

coming from the sea, and he stared hard at them. With a shock he knew what it was. "Those aren't clouds, Pete! That's smoke! That's a fire!"

They turned at the bottom of the hill. Pete looked ahead, bending to see better through the windshield. The smoke billowed up out of the estate like a tornado, dark and angry, and now they could see the red of the flames licking up at the sky.

"Holy God!" Pete said. "You're right! What the hell could be burning like that?"

"The estate!" Tommy cried. "That's the old estate on fire! My friends Joel and Little Horse live up there!"

15

TWO FIRE TRUCKS were stalled in the narrow road outside the gates. Behind the iron gates the avenue of the palm trees burned like two rows of huge torches. A pair of firemen hacked at the old padlock on the gates with an axe. A helicopter flew in circles over the fire, passing in and out of the billowing clouds of black smoke. The whirring of the twin helicopter propellers, the whining of the fire trucks, the shouts of the firemen, the police trying to direct traffic, and from afar the scream of more sirens on the way combined to make the narrow street a place of deafening noise.

The police waved Pete and Tommy off the road. They left the truck on a side street and walked in.

"No spectators," a policeman ordered. "Keep the street clear."

"I live here!" Tommy said.

"Where?"

"Up there in the apartment building. My mom will be waiting for me."

The officer looked at Tommy to see if he was lying, and then at Pete. "All right. Go on up."

People stood along the roofs of the apartment buildings. A small crowd had gathered near the humming fire trucks. Pete and Tommy pushed their way through. Beyond the crowd there was another group of police officers. They stood in a circle, guns out, guarding a half dozen young rough-looking boys. The boys were sitting in the road, hands on their heads, legs crossed.

There was no sign of either Joel or Little Horse.

"Listen to that, you little morons," a policeman shouted at the boys in the road. "You hear that burning? That's what you started. We ought to take you and fling you back into the fire."

The crowd muttered angrily in agreement.

"You gonna burn us out, you creeps," a man yelled through the ring of policemen. "If the buildings go, everything I own goes with them!" He tore at his hair, his eyes wild, and then he flung himself on the policemen, trying to get at the boys. They looked scared. Their eyes were wide with fear. They sat there not saying anything, waiting to be taken away in the police cars that could be heard wailing closer.

"Arsonists!" screamed a woman.

"Everybody BACK!" the policemen shouted. "BACK!

Go collect your valuables. If we can't control the fire, these buildings will have to be evacuated."

The crowd grew more angry. They shouted at the boys in the road.

"Back!" the policemen ordered. "All of you. Get going!"

"This damn gate is rusted together," one of the firemen shouted. "We'll have to pull it off."

Working quickly, they tied a rope through the bars of the gate, fixed it to the first truck, and waved to the driver. The siren rose to a high scream as he warned the people to get out of the street, and then the truck jerked forward. The gate bent. It didn't come off.

Tommy felt a hand on his shoulder. He turned to find his mother behind him. "Tommy. Thank God you're safe!"

Pete was looking the other way. "Will you look at that guy?" he said, pointing up at the helicopter circling above the fire. "Man, that takes guts!"

"Pete," Susan Bridges said and, even though she spoke softly, Pete seemed to hear her voice above all the racket, for he stiffened and kept on looking up at the circling bird. "Pete . . ." she repeated.

He turned slowly. He looked different to Tommy, shy and hurt. "Hi," he said, like a kid out on his first date.

Susan Bridges reached out and touched Pete on the arm, and he stepped back half a pace as though she'd burned him. Then to Tommy's shock Pete blushed. "Thank you, Pete. I was worried half out of my mind."

Pete smiled. "You should have figured out where he'd come," Pete said slowly. "If either of you were in trouble, I'd expect you to come . . ." He didn't finish. Tommy's mom and Pete just stared at each other for a long time, and then tears came into his mom's eyes and Pete looked away quickly.

"You didn't go out with Mort again last night?" Tommy asked.

His mom looked at Pete, who was studying the helicopter again. It swooped closer, the blades whirring in a frenzy above their heads. The wind from the whirring blades bent the branches of the trees, ripping off leaves and scattering them along the street, then it swung away again toward the fire, disappearing into the smoke from the flaming palm trees.

"No," his mom said. "I may be dumb, but I'm not that dumb."

"Lots of people have been doing dumb things lately," Pete said, staring into the distance. "There must be something in the air."

The gates tore away from their posts, dragging along in the dirt behind the fire truck. The firemen rushed forward to untie the ropes while the siren wailed. The boys in the street covered their ears with their hands. They looked at each other, at the policemen guarding them, at the fire trucks with the flames of the estate behind, and they saw what they had done.

The first truck moved forward with the men hanging on its side. It nudged its way through the gate into the driveway where the avenue of palm trees burned fiercely in the hot morning sky.

"Back. Everyone back," the policemen shouted. They pulled the boys to their feet and hustled them toward a black van with barred windows, marked POLICE in white letters. The fire truck moved into the fiery tunnel of trees. The people on the roofs of the apartments cheered.

But the cheers had hardly started when they died, the sound of the voices falling away until all that could be heard was the roaring of the fire. Before their eyes a large tree cracked, bent inward, and hung there suspended above the truck with the flaming fronds reaching like fingers of fire down to the men on the truck.

"Run!" the chief ordered. "It's coming down." The men leaped from the trapped truck, racing back down the driveway as the ruined tree cracked like a gunshot and fell across the truck.

"My God," said Susan Bridges. "Those men were almost trapped in there!"

Another tree came down with a roar. From the gate all that was visible was the rear of the fire truck engulfed in flames.

A voice from the sky rasped, "Leave the area please! Proceed to your apartments, collect your valuables, and leave the area."

The helicopter swung out of the smoke, blades throbbing like a beating heart.

"This area must be evacuated," said the loudspeaker in the helicopter. "Leave the area immediately."

Waves of heat beat down upon the people from the spinning blades. The crowd hunched almost as one person, squinting their eyes to look up into the sky.

The police came forward with their own bullhorn. "You are ordered to proceed calmly to your residences, remove only valuables that can be carried, and leave the area."

The crowd ran in every direction.

"Calmly," shouted the police, but they were ignored.

"What will happen to the estate?" Tommy asked.

"It'll burn to the earth," Pete said. He took Tommy's mother by the elbow. "Let's get your stuff."

"But the people in there!" Tommy protested.

"There aren't any people in there, son," said the nearest policeman. "The little brats who set the fire are on their way to the slammer right now."

"But Joel and Little Horse!" Tommy protested.

The policeman scowled. "Out of the area, son," he said.

Tommy looked at the fire. The engine was engulfed in flames. The towers of smoke hid everything but the flaming palms. The canyon was a cauldron of smoke and flame. An animal shrieked high in the canyon, the thin screams piercing the morning air with primitive terror.

Tommy knew as sure as he knew his name that Joel and Little Horse were still in there. He looked frantically about for help. The firemen were emptying their hand extinguishers onto the burning truck. The police were moving down the avenue, arms linked, to clear the crowd. Pete had his arm around Susan Bridges, helping her out of the way. Tommy took a deep breath, ducked under the arm of the nearest policeman, and sped through the gates of the estate. Ahead of him the falling palm trees were piled in a huge bonfire on the fire truck where the red paint was exploding in blisters.

"COME BACK HERE, KID!"

"Pete! Oh, my God, look . . . !"

Tommy hopped off the path, brushing past the scorched branches. He felt the heat of the fire on his cheeks, like a blast from a furnace. If he could get by the truck he might be able to climb the canyon. The brush would be on fire, but the road that wound up to the gazebo might be safe. If he could get up there he could find Joel and Little Horse, he could help them.

"COME BACK HERE!" the voice screamed again, and Tommy heard shouting. There was a fracas behind him. He heard someone pursuing him. He ran faster through the dry brush, moving fast along the path he'd spent all summer exploring. His pursuer crashed along behind him. As he breathed he drew the smoke into his lungs. He coughed, clutching at his chest, staggered, and forced himself to go on.

An explosion tore the air, followed by a blast of hot air that tossed him forward; he rolled over in the tinder-dry brush while sparks flew all about. He struck a rock with his shoulder, lost consciousness, and came to a minute later with a body leaning across him.

"You all right?" a voice asked. It was Pete.

They helped each other to their feet. The canyon was filling with black smoke. It was as thick as fog rolling backward to where the canyon walls met. All the palms were down. The lower brush was a carpet of fire.

"What was that?"

"The truck went up," Pete said. "We can't get back that way."

"They're up there," Tommy said. "They *are*, Pete. I know."

Pete didn't argue. That was one of the great things about Pete. He accepted what a kid said. Instead, he looked up in the direction that Tommy pointed, above the smoke, to the distant gazebo.

"The fire will be up there soon," Pete said. "If they're there, we've gotta get them out. Why aren't they coming down?"

"Maybe they're hurt," Tommy said. "Those kids who set the fire have been after them."

"All right," Pete said. "We go up. You know the way. You lead."

They heard the helicopter before they saw it. The blades of the machine fanned the air as it descended out of the towers of smoke, blowing waves of scorching air at them. "You will proceed to the nearest clear area," the voice of the bullhorn grated. "Repeat: you will proceed to the nearest clear space for recovery. That is an order."

The machine hovered fifty feet above them to see if they were going to do as they were ordered.

"Pete," Tommy urged in case Pete waved. "Little Horse and Joel . . ."

"Get going," Pete said. "We've got to get out of here in a hurry. Everything in this canyon is going to burn."

Tommy ran. The fire was creeping forward like a tide, small sparks at first that landed in the dried grass where they crackled, sending out waves of tiny sparks of their own, then the smaller bushes, which lit the lower branches of the trees. As the heat increased and the leaves dried out, the trees burst into flame, the branches reaching up like hands clawing at the sky. The bark exploded off the tree trunks. Panic-stricken, the birds flew in circles, calling to each other with maddened cries.

Where the path branched to the left a rattler and her nest of babies had found shelter on the path. The mother was reared back on her coil, rattle shaking like a drum, while the six-inch vipers rolled in the dirt looking for relief from the heat.

Pete grabbed a palm frond and plunged it into a burning bush until the leaves caught fire. He held the frond before him, approaching the snake, which reared back to strike again and again at the flames. Pete scooped the snake up and flung her wide off the path.

"Run!" he called, and Tommy leaped across the coils of the writhing snakes.

The trees crackled as they made their way up to the road on the canyon rim. They were both coughing when they at last came out of the thickest part of the smoke and stood on the road. Below them the canyon was a sea of fire.

"It's going to climb the canyon walls, leap the road, and spread into the hills," Pete said.

The copter came around again, the blades beating the air angrily as it hovered off to the side of the road. "YOU

(131)

ARE ORDERED TO PROCEED TO THE NEAREST CLEARED SPACE AND REMAIN THERE FOR PICKUP," the voice boomed at them. They could see the men in the copter now. A pilot held the machine level with them just above the fire. Beside him was a fire marshal holding the bullhorn.

"He must be crazy," Pete said. "We can't go down there again. We'd be burned alive."

Ignoring the furious looks of the marshal, they turned up the road. They made slow progress. The road was steep and they were out of breath. Unable to come closer because of the canyon wall, the copter stayed out above the fire. The fire marshal had realized that it was impossible for them to go down. They had to go up. He held the horn in his lap. His face was red with anger. After a minute he gave an order to the pilot, and the copter swung away over the flaming trees.

The first tendrils of smoke crept up onto the road. Small animals, gophers and rabbits, ran out of the bushes up the side of the canyon. The sky above was slate gray.

"Man, that storm better get here," Pete said, "or these hills will go up like firewood."

They couldn't see any sign of rain clouds. The canyon floor was hidden by smoke. The gate and the burning engine were lost in flame. As they ran they saw the roofline of the apartment buildings and the people lined up along the edge like tiny toy soldiers. The helicopter came back and took another swing over the smoke, but the bullhorn stayed quiet.

(132)

The roar of the fire was the only sound to be heard. Below them it bellowed like a trapped beast. Trees crashed down and the heat rippled the air.

The gazebo was close now. Two more bends and they'd be there.

Tommy staggered. He fell to his knees coughing. His skin felt dry, as though he'd been out in the sun too long. His hair crackled like the dry underbrush. Pete grabbed him with one arm and hauled him to his feet. "Push yourself harder," he ordered the boy. "You'll get another wind soon."

Tommy's lungs felt scorched. His eyes watered. The air he took in burned down into his lungs. He forced himself to go on.

"Take shallow breaths," Pete said. "We'll get there."

The road seemed to stretch on and on. Tommy put one foot in front of the other, following Pete as he marched step by step up the last hundred yards, and then they were above the fire, and a cool breeze blew on them from the other side of the hills. They stood on the edge of the clearing, breathing deeply the cooler air. Pete looked about, up at the sky first and away up the coast. "Look," he said, pointing. "There's the storm." Tommy followed the direction of his finger, and there to the north were black rain clouds. Pete looked down over the ridge into the canyon where the smoke was rising like a tide, almost as dark as the rain clouds. "It's going to be a race," he said. "Let's get your friends and get out of here."

Where the vegetable garden had been, the young plants were trampled into the mud. The clothesline was torn from the trees. Everywhere were scattered the few belongings that Joel and Little Horse had gathered.

"They trashed it," Tommy said.

"Something happened up here," Pete said. "That's for sure."

Tommy went up the steps to the gazebo. Joel had closed it to give them some shelter from the wind. The sides had been torn away. Inside, Little Horse's books on Indian living were torn to shreds. Joel's faded blue shirt had been ripped in two and dropped in the center of the floor.

"Maybe they killed them," Tommy whispered.

"No bodies," Pete said. "This looks like they got mad because they couldn't find them. Is there anywhere your friends could hide?"

Tommy thought about the night he'd run all the way up the canyon to get away from Mort. "There's the lookout," he said. He ran across the clearing to the lookout. The bushes were still in place. He pushed them aside, calling, "Joel? Little Horse?" Behind the bushes the grass was flat, but there was no sign of either of them.

Pete came and stood beside Tommy. "Not here?"

"No," said Tommy. He was worried. "They *must* be here, Pete. They *must* be. They never go anywhere except Thursday."

"Thursday?" asked Pete.

"Unemployment day," Tommy said. "That's the day Little Horse gets his check. They go to the store that day, then they come back here."

"Maybe they changed their routine," Pete said, and

the way he said it Tommy could tell he was getting mad. The smoke was rising in the canyon. The flames leaped like animals themselves now, setting one part and then another of the brush afire. The fire line was creeping up the canyon like water rising in a tub. "Maybe this time they decided to go to a movie or something."

"No!" said Tommy firmly. "They're here somewhere. They were afraid of the crazies from the boulevard and they knew they were looking for them, so they hid out. But they wouldn't go to a show. They'd never leave the clearing unguarded. They haven't got anywhere else to go. It's all they've got, Pete."

The voice came from a long way off. They weren't sure at first that they had heard anything. They both looked around, searching for the caller.

"Tommy!" the voice called again, faint and far away.

Pete looked over the edge. "Oh, my God!" he said.

Far below in the brush just above the fire line were two figures. The smoke blew all about them, hiding them for minutes at a time.

"Tommy, help us!"

Briefly the smoke cleared. Little Horse lay sprawled on his back with Joel kneeling beside him.

"He's hurt," Pete said.

"We'll have to rescue them."

The smoke covered the figures again. Pete said, "That fire is just a few feet away from them." He looked around. "Take off your shirt," he ordered.

Tommy did as he was told. Pete led him over to the water tap Joel had rigged into a shower. "Stand under that," Pete ordered, turning on the tap full blast. "Soak your clothes well, especially your shirt."

Tommy stood under the cool water until his pants, his shoes, his hair were soaking wet. He held his shirt up, letting it soak up water. Then he put the shirt back on while Pete stood under the tap.

As they ran back to the canyon edge the helicopter came in low above them, the blades beating a deafening rhythm in the sky. "You are ordered to remain where you are!" the bullhorn shouted. "We are coming in for a landing."

"Over you go," Pete said to Tommy, ignoring the bullhorn. He swung Tommy wide of the rim and let him down carefully to the next foothold. "Hold onto the bushes. I'll be right behind you."

The canyon side was as steep as a cliff. The scrub bushes were rooted deep to withstand the Santa Ana winds. They made good handholds. Tommy let himself down holding tight to the bushes, scrabbling for a foothold as he made his way closer and closer to where they had last seen the two figures. The heat blasted them. His clothes dried out. Dirt from Pete's boots scattered past him, striking him on the neck. He could hear the thunderous noise of the copter coming in for a landing in the clearing.

The copter blades beat the smoke back. There right ahead of Tommy were Joel and Little Horse. Little Horse was pale. "He's broken his leg," Joel called.

Tommy and Pete climbed down to the ledge. "They tried to smoke us out by starting the fire," Joel said. "They came up and trashed the place, but we hid. Then they started the fire at the gate, thinking we'd run down the road. They were waiting for us at the end, so we went over the edge. But Little Horse, he don't have much experience in climbing, and he fell and broke his leg. I sure am glad to see you!"

"We'll get you out of here," Tommy said. "Won't we, Pete?"

"You Pete?" Joel asked. "Man, from what Tommy says, you can practically walk on water."

"This might be harder," Pete told him. "How are we going to get an injured man up that canyon?"

Above them the bullhorn spoke. "How many of you are there?"

They looked up. The fire marshal stood at the canyon rim with the pilot.

"There's four," Pete called. "One injured."

"Do you have room for a stretcher?" the bullhorn asked.

"Send it down," Pete answered him.

"There's a flare coming down. Light it."

The marshal dropped an object over the side. Pete reached out to grab it. He missed. The flare bounced down into the flames. The smoke was blowing back up to the ledge.

"Another," Pete called. "Joel, you steady me."

Joel jumped up from beside Little Horse and took hold of Pete around the waist. Pete leaned out from the ledge as far as he could. "Now," he called.

The second flare came down. The smoke blew in thin clouds all about. Pete snatched the flare out of the air as it fell.

"Light it," the bullhorn ordered.

Pete lodged the flare in a crack on the side of the canyon. He lit it. The flare burned bright orange in the gathering smoke.

"Don't anybody move," Pete said. "You could fall over the edge easily. Nothing could help you then." He knelt down beside Little Horse. "His breathing's uneven. He needs oxygen."

They heard the stretcher being lowered down the cliff. It came down at the end of a rope through the smoke. Pete undid it. "All right," he said. "We'll have to lift him onto it all at once. As it is, he's in shock." Pete was working fast undoing the stretcher, rolling it out, retying the rope so that it was attached to both ends.

The unseen bullhorn called down to them. "When the injured man is on the stretcher, pull on the ropes. We will raise him."

"You two take his shoulders," Pete said. "I'll take his legs." He carefully tried to straighten the broken leg. Little Horse cried out. "When I say," Pete said. Joel and Tommy took Little Horse under the shoulders. "Now!" Pete said, and the three of them picked up the stricken man and lifted him onto the stretcher. Little Horse screamed in pain.

They strapped him down rapidly. Pete stood up and pulled on the ropes. Nothing happened for several seconds, then the stretcher jerked upward off the ledge. "I'll have to climb behind it to steady it," Pete said. "Can you two make it up on your own?"

"Sure can," Joel replied, and as Pete climbed up the canyon behind the stretcher, he said to Tommy, "That's some guy."

"I told you," Tommy said.

The stretcher inched up the canyon. Pete stayed just below it, to help the burden over the snags. Tommy and Joel climbed up by themselves. Behind them the fire crept over the ledge to lick at their feet.

Pete helped the stretcher up over the rim of the canyon. The fire marshal and the pilot who had been pulling on the ropes collapsed panting onto the ground with the sweat running down their faces. They were up again in a minute. "That fire's going to be over the rim in a few minutes," the marshal said. "We've got to get out of here." He looked over the hills toward the airport. "They're going to drop about ten tons of chemicals into the canyon, to try to hold it."

Three dark specks on the horizon were the bombers taking off from the airfield.

Pete and the marshal lifted the stretcher with Little Horse and carried it to the copter. The pilot leaped in and turned over the engine, and the blades turned once slowly, then rapidly, beating the bushes flat with the force of the air currents. Bending low, Pete and the marshal put Little Horse into the copter.

"There won't be room for all of us," said the marshal.

"Take the boys," Pete said. "I'll wait."

"No, Pete," said Tommy. "I'll stay with you."

In answer Pete lifted Tommy off his feet and chucked him into the copter. "Don't argue, boy. Time's wasting." He helped Joel up. Before Tommy could make any further protest, Pete stepped back. The copter lifted off out across the burning canyon. Tommy strained to see. Pete stood alone in the clearing with the fire eating its way up toward him.

"Pete!" he called.

"Sit down, kid," the marshal ordered him. "We'll be going back." He looked at the approaching bombers, larger now and closer. "If they don't get there first," he muttered to the pilot. "They won't wait to see what's below when they drop that stuff."

They flew low over the fire toward the entrance of the estate. The lower part of the canyon was a charred mass. The fire engine was a twisted mass of blackened steel. At the rear of the canyon the fire burned furiously. They circled the roof of the first apartment building. A crude circle was marked in white chalk dust. Out of range stood a few people in everyday clothes, a few fireman, and two white-coated medics.

"In we go," said the pilot, lowering the copter over the circle. The machine bumped down on the roof in a rough landing, and before the blades had stopped, the medics were running to the helicopter door. They took hold of the stretcher with Little Horse and lifted it out. Tommy was helped down by the waiting firemen, and then Joel.

His mother ran out of the small crowd of people." Tommy," she cried, hugging him to her. "Thank heavens. Thank heavens." She looked around. "Where's Pete?"

Joel had gone with the stretcher. They were taking it in the roof top down to the elevator. "He's still up there," Tommy said. "There wasn't room."

Susan Bridges spun around to look back at the fire. The flames were over the canyon rim now. From here it looked as though the clearing itself was on fire. The marshal shouted, "Out of the way. We have to go back."

Looking in the same direction as Susan Bridges, the pilot said, "I don't know, Sam. I don't think I can take her in if the fire's there."

"We'll have to try to take him out by ladder," the marshal said, hopping up into the cabin.

The blades spun again, the crowd stepped back, and the copter lifted off. The drone of the bombers was close. They could see the planes coming in over the hillside.

Tommy's mom squeezed him hard against her. She was crying. They watched while the helicopter headed back over the fire. It went over the rim of the canyon, hovered over the clearing, spun away. "They've left him!" Susan Bridges cried.

The helicopter made a circle and went back in again, trailing the rope ladder. The pilot lowered the plane as low as he could. From the roof they saw the tiny figure of Pete reaching up to take hold of the lower rungs of the rope. The ladder danced in the air, eluding him. The bombers were over the fire now. The watchers could read the markings on the wings. The faraway figure got hold of the first rung of the ladder and pulled himself up until his feet had a hold. He hung onto the lower rungs while the helicopter swung away from the fire again, out across the burning estate, dragging the tail of rope with the tiny figure clutching on for his life.

The bombers released their load, and a wave of foaming chemicals poured out of the sky over the fire. A wall of steam rose up, hiding everything.

The crowd on the roof was silent. They held their breath to see if the copter had made it with its burden. Through the clouds of smoke and steam they heard the throbbing, and then out of the mists came the machine still carrying its passenger at the end of the rope ladder. The pilot lowered him above the roof until he could jump. Pete leaped from the ladder, sagged to his knees, and stayed there. The medics ran for him. The helicopter swung away.

Pete waved the medics off. "I'm fine, I'm fine," he said. Susan let go of Tommy. She ran forward. Pete stood up and she ran into his arms. "Pete," she sobbed.

Pete held onto her tight. "Hey," he murmured. "I'm the one that had the fright, remember?" Then he kissed her.

Much later when it was night and the crowds were gone, the fire engines, the bombers leaving the fire sputtering and steaming, and they were back in their own apartment, Pete said, "Well, I guess I should go."

Tommy's mom had cooked a meal for the three of them the way she used to. For a few hours it had been like old times. But then as the hours passed, Pete and Tommy's mom had gotten awkward with each other. There had been long silences as though they didn't know what to say. One or the other of them would start to talk suddenly, too loud and too fast, and the good feeling was gone.

Pete stood up. "It's been . . . good seeing you, Susan."

Tommy could see that his mom was close to tears. But she tried not to show that. "You too, Pete," she said. "You look . . . well."

"Yeah . . ." Pete said. "Uh . . . you two come up and see me in Santa Barbara, you hear?"

"We'll do that," Susan Bridges said, and now her eyes were shining with water.

Pete had his hand on the doorknob. He held onto it for a long time. Susan Bridges turned away so he wouldn't see that she was crying. Pete took a deep breath. "Uh . . . this kind of scares me . . ." he began. "But . . . uh . . . you wouldn't marry me, would you?"

Tommy couldn't believe he'd heard right. He looked at his mom to see if she'd heard Pete. Susan Bridges was staring at Pete as though she didn't know him. The seconds dragged out. Pete looked embarrassed and uncomfortable.

Tommy yelled, "Say yes, dummy!"

His mom burst out laughing. "Yes, dummy," she said to Pete. "Oh, yes, Pete. Yes."

Pete was laughing too. "Say," he said to Tommy, "that's no way to talk to the woman I love."

He walked over to Susan and took her in his arms. "I don't have anything to offer you, Sooze," he said.

"You've got all I need," she said.

That's the way they were standing when the door flew

open. Twink Mondragon stood in the doorway, as mad as a wet hen. "What's all this about you standing Mort up?" she demanded.

Susan Bridges had her arms around Pete. "I'm getting married, Twink," she said.

"You must be Pete," Twink said.

"That's right. Who are you?"

Twink ignored him. She spoke to Susan Bridges. "You can't have that and a career too," she said.

"I'll settle for this," Susan Bridges replied, looking up at Pete.

"Men!" said Twink. "None of you are any good," and she slammed out.

Pete laughed. "She may be right."

"I'll take my chances," said Tommy's mom.

16

IN THE MORNING they packed their suitcases and carried them down to the truck. Susan Bridges took the key to the landlady and told her they wouldn't need it anymore. The storm had hit in the night. All that was left of the estate was a black scar in the hills.

They stopped by the hospital. Joel was visiting Little Horse in the trauma ward. Little Horse had had his leg set and he looked much better. Joel had been treated for smoke inhalation.

"I gotta thank you," Little Horse said to Tommy.

"Thank Pete," Tommy said. "He saved you."

Little Horse stuck out his hand. "Thanks, man."

"You're welcome, Little Horse," Pete said, shaking the hand.

Little Horse blushed. "All that stuff, all that Indian stuff, that was dumb. I'm no Indian. I'm a cabbie."

"Lot of people been dumb lately," Pete said. "Me included."

"We're going home with Pete," Tommy burst out. "Pete and Mom are getting married."

Joel said, "I know one person that's going to make real happy," and he looked at Tommy.

"What are you going to do now?" Pete asked.

"I thought maybe I'd try San Francisco," Little Horse said. "The kid's folks told the police they don't want him back. I'll take him up there with me. I can get a job hacking, he can go to school, maybe make something of himself."

Tommy could see that that pleased Joel.

"Listen," Pete said. "Santa Barbara's right on the way to San Francisco. You two stop off with us for a few days, you hear?"

Little Horse and Joel smiled broadly. "O.K.!"

"Promise?" said Tommy.

"Honest Injun," said Little Horse, and everyone laughed.

The day was bright and clear. Tommy sat between Pete and his mom in the old truck, looking ahead up the coast, feeling better than he had felt in his whole life. Out on the ocean the waves shone in the sunlight. Tommy felt warm all over. Living could be tough work, he thought, but if you were lucky, sometimes, not always, but sometimes everything worked out just as you had hoped it would and that made everything, all the tough times, O.K.

Then the truck rattled around the last bend, and there

was Santa Barbara: the oil derricks with their spindle legs sunk in the ocean, the surfers out on the waves floating on their boards like a school of fish, the white sand beach, and the town spread across the hills. Out on the horizon were the Channel Islands, where by straining hard he could just make out the fishing fleet trawling the channel.

"Hurry, Pete," he cried. "We're missing the catch!"

STUART BUCHAN is a Canadian citizen who was born in Australia and educated in Singapore, Great Britain, Canada, and the United States. He now lives in California. The author of a novel, *Fleeced*, Mr. Buchan has also written articles and reviews for several newspapers. He holds a graduate degree in English and has been a teacher of remedial reading. *When We Lived with Pete* is Mr. Buchan's first book for young readers.